His face was a pale blur in the semi-darkness, and Vince heard the rasp of his breathing. A man could recklessly burn up his strength and spend it in a few furious moments, or he could spread it out to cover the situation. Vince decided Morgan had saved but little. He pushed off the good leg, getting leverage behind the blow. He sledged Morgan full in the mouth, and Morgan reeled backwards, spitting blood and curses. Vince did not give him time to recover. He rained in blows, and each fist was a sharp edge chipping away an additional bit of strength. He was hit in return, but Morgan's fists were losing their kick. He slugged Morgan in the face, and Morgan clawed open handed at him. The fingers of a hand closed on his shirt, and the front of it went with the raking grab.

Vince hit him again, and he was punching at an almost defenseless man. Morgan sobbed for breath, and his weary arms kept sagging on him. He stumbled under a punishing blow to the belly and somehow remained on his feet. He reeled and staggered, his hands pawing blindly before him.

"You can call it off n   ," Vince said. "Or I'll finish it."

Charter Westerns by Giles A. Lutz

THE WILD QUARRY

GILES A. LUTZ

CHARTER BOOKS, NEW YORK

THE WILD QUARRY

A Charter Book / published by arrangement with
the author

PRINTING HISTORY
Ace edition published 1961
Charter edition / April 1985

ISBN: 0-441-88852-6

Charter Books are published by The Berkley Publishing Group,
200 Madison Avenue, New York, New York 10016.
PRINTED IN THE UNITED STATES OF AMERICA

1

THE TOWN was as Vince Carwin remembered it, gray and beaten under the vagaries of the New Mexico weather. He stopped his mount on the rise above the town and stared at it, old memories rushing in to fill his head. Ten years—almost half of his life—was a long time to be gone, and the pull of childhood recollections was a strong tide sweeping him back.

What one remembered best about a town was its people. A building had no individuality, and it was only the person who inhabited it who gave it life and warmth. He recalled old man Miller, who ran the saddle shop—his crusty, crabby exterior foreboding to a kid, until he learned of the soft heart underneath. He remembered cutting his finger with a sharp knife Miller gave him to use. He thought of Hamilton, who owned the general store. Sometimes Hamilton gave him a piece of penny candy, and other times he ran him out of the store. He remembered Marshal Goddard stalking the streets, his harsh face never softening with a smile.

The kids kept their pranks to a minimum at just the mention of Goddard's name.

The sorrel danced with restless impatience. Vince leaned over and patted its neck. It was only half broken, knowing man and his touch for less than three weeks. Its instincts and yearnings still turned toward the wild freedom it once had known.

"Easy, boy," Vince said soothingly. A man stayed alert to the sorrel's moods, or he would find himself on his butt in the dust. But it was the best advertisement he could have brought with him. It was big-barreled and clean-limbed, topping sixteen hands. Its burnished coat shone in the morning sun, and the fire in its eye would catch and gladden the heart of any cavalry officer. Vince hoped Captain Simas was waiting for him with a contract for a hundred more just like the sorrel.

He looked at the town again before he lifted the reins. A town was names—good and bad names, and his head was filled with them. He had known them through a kid's eyes, and now, he would be looking at them through a man's eyes. Whether or not there was change did not concern him. He came here to pick up no old threads. But he did wish Simas had picked some other town as a meeting place.

He swore softly and put the sorrel into motion. He rode easily, his tall, spare body giving with the action of the horse. His smooth face was the color of a saddle left out for years in the wind and sun and rain, and his body had a hard, whiplash quality to it. His eyes were gray, deep-set and a little withdrawn, the eyes of a man who had grown up too much alone.

An old black Colt .44 rode at his hip, and a rifle was in its scabbard under his knee. In 1885 men didn't use guns as readily to settle their troubles as they had done ten years earlier. The law and the courts were replacing the guns, and Vince was not too sure the change was a good one. The reasons for shooting some men were as evident as they had ever been, but the courts too many times over-looked those reasons and protected the wrong men.

He shook his head at his thoughts. He was here to avenge nothing. He was here on business and for no other reason. Anything he could do would never re-make the past. The war between squatters and big ranchers had been over for a sizeable number of years, and he had no desire to blow on old embers, even though his father had been indirectly killed.

But he found it almost impossible to push out old thoughts—they clung with barbed feet, prodding and irritating a man. He could remember the night his father died as vividly as though it were happening now. A twelve-year-old boy stood at the door of a dying man's bedroom, listening to his harsh breathing. Each rasping breath further twisted that boy's guts, leaving him more terrified. Half a hundred times that night his mother had said, "Vince, see if the doctor is coming," and as many times he had stood outside the cold winter night's air, straining to hear or see an approaching buggy.

The doctor never came, and looking back, Vince doubted that it would have done any good. Pneumonia was a swift and merciless killer, and its hold was too advanced for any doctor to combat it.

He had been almost glad when that terrible, rasp-

ing breathing stopped. But then—what was worse
—his mother's crying started. The dry sobbing
went on and on. The tears had been wrung out of
her during the days of her husband's illness. There
was nothing a small boy could say or do to comfort
her.

A dozen times during that awful night his mother
had cried out, "Dobie Nerich did this!"

It had only further bewildered the boy. How did
Nerich have anything to do with his father dying in
that room? She had tried to explain it to him by
asking, "Do you remember the night, ten days ago,
when the haystacks were on fire?"

He remembered that—the orange balls of light
mushrooming into towering flames of brilliance
that lit up the whole country. He remembered his
father jumping out of bed and running outside
without waiting to fully dress. New Mexico winters
could be cold, and after the exertion of unsuc-
cessfully fighting four separate fires came the reaction. How his father had shivered! Even the whisky
and the irons—heated on the stove, wrapped in
blankets and placed beside him in bed—could not
stop it. "We're ruined, Mamie," his father said.
"That was the winter's feed for the animals."

The exposure and the reaction opened wide the
doors for pneumonia, and his mother blamed Dobie
Nerich. Vince was with her when she talked to
Marshal Goddard about it. "The sheriff wouldn't
listen to you, would he, Mamie?" Goddard asked.

"He's a friend of Nerich," she said bitterly.

Goddard shook his head. "You're making accusations without proof. You didn't see Dobie there, did you?"

The lie had trembled on her lips; then she shook her head in dull defeat. "No," she admitted. "I didn't see him. But he did it or had it done. You know he's driven out other small ranchers."

"I might think it," Goddard corrected her. "But that's a long way from proving it."

She could find no proof, and she left the country soon after her husband's death. The hardships for a woman and twelve-year-old son had been too great, and those and the bitterness had driven her away as surely as whips. She had died when Vince was fifteen, and practically her last words were, "He needs killing." The intensity of her hating had scared Vince as a kid—and try as he might, Vince had never been quite able to share it.

It brought its corresponding sense of guilt that he could not hate a name. As a kid he had tried to puzzle through it. If anyone did wrong in town, Goddard punished them. He knew that. But Goddard had done nothing to Nerich. It was always possible his mother could be wrong.

Anyway, he was not returning with hatred flaming his blood. Vaguely he remembered Nerich as a big man with a heavy beard. After ten years he was not even sure he would recognize Nerich if he saw him.

After his mother's death he had wandered, finally joining up with a bunch of wild horse hunters. He found a solace and contentment with them. They were a lonely breed, spending most of their time in the vast emptiness the wild horse inhabited. It was hard and often dangerous work and meagerly rewarded. Now Vince was on his own, and this tentative deal he had with Simas was the biggest that had dropped into his hands.

He was at the head of the main street; he shrugged the thoughts of the past away. There was still enough kid in him to want to make an entrance. He told himself that Simas might be watching, that he wanted to show off the sorrel. He grinned at his reasoning, seeing the lies in it.

He raked spurs the length of the sorrel's barrel and heard its outraged rush of breath. The steel-like muscles bunched under him, and the horse was immediately in full stride. It had a sweet action as it thundered down the street, its long clean legs reaching and scissoring distance behind them.

Men were pulled out onto the wooden walks by the noise of the sorrel's run, and Vince threw back his head and howled sheer exuberance. He jerked the sorrel into a skidding stop and swung off before it was fully halted, running a dozen steps beside it and hauling on the reins. His face was alive with eagerness, for he was in his element. Vince Carwin knew and loved horses, and only when he was handling them did his inward shyness disappear.

With he finished tying the sorrel to a rack, he was breathing hard, and he turned to face the knot of watching men. His face went wooden under their stares, and he warily watched them. He was never quite at ease in a town. He always felt like an animal that had been caught too far away from its hole.

One of the watching men said, "You've got a wild one there, Mister. He'll break those reins."

Vince glanced at the sorrel. It jerked back on the reins, its eyes rolling, its wicked little pike ears alternately raising and lowering. The wooden tie-rack quivered under the savage force exerted against it. This was the way the cavalry wanted them. No recruit ever learned to ride on some mild, spirit-broken animal.

"Not those reins," Vince said briefly. He knew the leather he had in them. He looked from face to face, hoping to see Simas. Some of these faces were vaguely familiar, but he did not attempt to put a name to them. He did not see Simas. He wondered if Simas had forgotten the agreement in Santa Fe to meet him here.

A bent shouldered, graying man came around the corner. He looked tired and beaten, and his step was heavy. A battered old black hat rode the back of his head, showing an unruly mass of iron-gray hair. No one was ever impressed by Ron Goddard's appearance, unless he looked at Goddard's eyes. Those blue eyes were set in a nest of crinkles and were eagle-sharp. Ten years had done nothing to diminish that sharpness. Vince remembered his kid-like awe of the marshal. He looked at the star, pinned to the threadbare vest. Perhaps a little of that awe still persisted.

Goddard's look was as probing as a coon's paw. He weighed Vince with those blue eyes and asked, "Don't I know you?"

He's as proddy as ever, Vince thought. Goddard used his authority like a club, swinging it first—

7

before the other man had a chance to get set. Vince suspected that was the reason he had lasted all these years. He kept on top of every and all situations. Goddard was not a popular man. A good lawman never was. He trod on too many toes.

Vince tried a grin and said, "Ron, that's a hell of a greeting for a homecoming."

Goddard squinted at him. "Vince Carwin," he said flatly. He had a remarkable memory for faces and names and the ability to put them together. "Back, and all growed up." His tone did not increase in friendliness.

"What are you doing here, Vince?"

Vince's face went stiff. He did not know what he expected—but surely more warmth than this. He started to say "that's my business," and held it. There had to be some reason for Goddard's attitude.

"I'm in the wild horse business, Ron. I'm to meet a Captain Simas here and make final arrangements to bring in a big bunch. I brought in that sorrel for him to look at. Have you seen him around?"

Goddard's eyes rested briefly on the sorrel. "Nice piece of horseflesh," he grunted. "Haven't seen him."

Then Simas was not in town, or Goddard would have known of it. Vince did not relish the thought of waiting in town several days for him.

Goddard's eyes never lost that weighing look. "You sure that's the only reason?"

Vince could not keep all the heat out of his voice. "What other reason would I have?"

8

"Dobie Nerich. He's in town."

Vince frowned at him. "That's just another name to me, Ron."

Goddard leaned toward him. "He took over the old homestead, after it went back."

"You're barking up the wrong tree," Vince said evenly. "I haven't spent all these years building up a hate. I've got my own business to attend to."

"Be sure it stays that way," Goddard warned. He took a step, stopped, and added as an afterthought, "Stay away from him. I will not have you starting any trouble in my town."

2

VINCE was tired, and his throat was dusty. He needed a drink or two to cushion the weariness and wash away the dust. The Black Butte Saloon was a block down the street, and he walked toward it.

He stepped inside. The soiled sawdust smelled of beer and old liquor, and the mirror above the back-bar had a million fly specks.

The bartender and another man were in the room. Vince did not know the bartender. The other man stood at the end of the bar, presenting only his profile. He was blocky with wide shoulders and a thick chest. His face was heavy and sun-blackened.

There was something familiar about that profile, and Vince stared at it.

The bartender broke into Vince's groping for a name to put to the profile by asking in a bored voice, "What'll it be, stranger?"

The bartender's question pulled the man's head around, while Vince was still staring at him. A puzzled frown wrinkled the man's forehead as though he should know Vince but could not quite place him.

Vince knew him. Hoyt Morgan was one of the few pleasant memories he had of this town. Morgan was three years older than Vince, and he had been Vince's self-appointed mentor. He kept the older boys off Vince, and he let him ride his pony. The days when he had worshipfully followed Hoyt Morgan loomed large in Vince's memory. He remembered that Morgan had not spared the blows, when he thought Vince had not been prompt enough in obeying some order. But no one else laid a hand on him.

"Hoyt," he cried and sprang forward.

Morgan did not take the extended hand. His face was round and chunky, and his eyes were as bright as bits of glass. Vince remembered those eyes as holding more warmth; then he thought their wariness could be because Morgan did not recognize him.

"Don't you know me, Hoyt?" He still held out his hand. "It's Vince Carwin."

"I'll be doggoned," Morgan said softly. He laughed, a low, amused sound. "You growed up, boy." He took Vince's hand and pumped it. Those bright, hard eyes traveled over Vince, not missing a thing.

"You the stranger who brought that sorrel in?" he asked. "A man was just in here talking about it."

Vince nodded. He thought he knew what was in Morgan's mind. The sorrel was something special. These old, worn clothes and the horse did not match at all.

Morgan asked, "You come back looking for a job?" It was a simple question, but there was a depth behind it—a wary waiting.

Vince shook his head. "I only expect to be here a day or so. I've got a job."

Morgan studied him. "You didn't come back to see any particular person?"

That was almost the same question Goddard asked. Vince pushed the irritating burr of it aside. "Sure," he said and paused. He did not miss the stiffening of Morgan's face. "You," he said and grunted. He thought the stiffening slackened. But the meeting had gone flat, and he thought mournfully, A man's memory plays him tricks.

Morgan appeared prosperous. His clothing was good, and his boots cost seventy-five dollars if they cost a cent. Vince did not miss the haste with which the bartender moved to serve Morgan. He had seen that kind of haste before. It was a haste born of fear and not of liking. He tried to push the wonder about it out of his mind.

It had been on his tongue to tell Morgan of his plans, and for some reason he held it. He could not say why, except that the meeting with Morgan was missing in something. Morgan seemed too carefully on guard. Perhaps that was it.

Vince turned the glass in his hand, making wet rings on the polished wood of the bar. "I've been wandering," he said slowly. "It isn't very profitable."

Morgan said sharply. "Did you expect to find a profit here? Your father's homestead went back a long time ago. If you had any ideas of picking it up, forget them."

"I haven't," Vince said curtly.

The silence between them grew until it was awkward. Morgan's face was showing anger under the weight of it. He flung a coin upon the bar and said, "Buy yourself another drink. I'll see you around."

Vince watched him push through the doors. He stared at the coin Morgan threw upon the bar and was tempted to throw it into the sawdust. He picked up his glass. The drink was paid for. He might as well finish it.

Morgan's boot heels drummed against the wooden walk, the rapidity of the beats saying this man was in a hurry—or upset. Or perhaps both. He paused to ask a man coming out of The Eagle's Nest Saloon, "Dobie still inside?"

The man nodded, and Morgan pushed by him. The place was in deep shadows after the brilliant sunlight, and for a moment he did not see Nerich. He spotted him at a back table and crossed to him. Nerich was a corpulent man. His table was as round as a full moon, and small, sly eyes peered out from the rolls of flesh. Thick lips were surrounded by a mass of luxuriant beard. One's first impression of Dobie Nerich was stomach and beard. That first impression missed the cunning in those small eyes, or the huge diamond upon his left hand. That cunning obtained that diamond for him, just as it obtained every other thing he wanted.

Nerich wiped his cuff across moist lips and asked, "What's eating on you?" Morgan made him a good man. He had a hunger for money, or rather the things money bought, and no compunctions as to how he got that money. He was a ragged-ass kid when Nerich picked him up—and now look at him.

Morgan said, "Vince Carwin is back."

A sharpness came into Nerich's eyes. "How well do you know him?"

"I used to cuff him around, when we were kids."

"Then why didn't you ask him why he came back?"

"I did. He said he wasn't interested in the homestead."

"Was he lying?"

"He could have been," Morgan grunted.

Nerich's eyes were reflective. Carwin came back for some reason, and he could be a menace. Dobie Nerich did not get as big as he was by overlooking the least menace.

"He's turned into the damned show-off," Morgan said. "He comes riding in here on that big sorrel—"

"Ah," Nerich broke in. "So he's the one who owns that horse. I wondered who it belonged to." His eyes gleamed. He wanted that horse, and what Dobie Nerich wanted he got. He ponderously hoisted himself to his feet. "Let's go talk to him. He might want to sell me that animal." He could also determine how much hostility was in Carwin.

Morgan thought of Vince Carwin's face. Vince would not sell that horse, unless he wanted to.

Morgan started to disagree with Nerich, then faintly smiled. A man was either with Dobie or against him. There was no middle ground. And Dobie's way was the way things usually happened.

He grinned and said, "I wouldn't be surprised if he sold, Dobie. And at your price, too."

3

A KNOT of men were gathered around the sorrel again, when Vince approached it.

He started to step off the walk, and Morgan said, "Vince, hold it a minute."

He turned, and a fat man moved toward him. Morgan followed the man, and there was something subservient in his manner that told Vince that Morgan worked for the fat man.

He waited, his face wooden. He did not miss the way men drew back to give the two passage. More of that fear grown respect, he thought.

The fat man stopped before him. His eyes went over Vince, and there was a feral quality to them that scraped Vince's skin. The man said in a wheezing voice, "Do you know me?"

Vince might not have, if the direct question had not prompted old memories. The remembrance of a heavy bearded man came back to him. Dobie Nerich. But the Dobie Nerich of ten years ago had not been so large. That huge body had now become gross. But the eyes were the same—sharp and hard and cruel.

His face picked up no expression. "I know you," he said.

Nerich put a hearty note in his voice. "What brings you back here, boy?"

"My business," Vince snapped.

Color flowed into Nerich's face, and Vince saw the hostility filling Morgan's eyes. His impression of a moment ago was right. Morgan was Nerich's man. Someone in the knot of watching men coughed nervously. Apparently, few people used that tone on Nerich.

Nerich held his temper and said, "That's a fine horse you have there."

"I think so." There was no more give in Vince's voice than the first time he spoke to Nerich.

Nerich struggled to hold his temper. "I'll buy him from you. If your price is right."

Vince's deliberate appraisal of him was as affronting as a slap in the face. "Nerich," he drawled. "You haven't enough money to buy that horse."

Someone in the crowd snickered, and Nerich's eyes turned raw and violent. Morgan made a forward motion, and Nerich's hand checked him. The man had control, for his eyes were almost calm again.

He said, "If you stay around long enough, you may learn to speak differently."

"Maybe," Vince said and stepped off the walk. He had no doubt as to where Morgan stood. That childhood association was gone and forgotten as far as Morgan was concerned. To hell with him, he thought with a sudden gust of anger. To hell with the rest of the town, too. Just as soon as Simas arrived and the arrangements could be made he would be on his way. He did not need, nor want, anything this town had to offer.

He jerked the knot in the reins free, gathered them up close in his left hand, and hauled the sorrel to him. He did not see Nerich move to the edge of the walk directly behind him. The sorrel's muscles were bunched, and Vince thought, I'll break your damned neck, if you pitch now.

The sorrel backed a couple of steps, and Vince followed him. He put his left foot into the stirrup and started to swing into the saddle. He heard a loud grunt behind him and a swishing sound as though something was swept through the air. But his back was turned, and he did not see what made the sound. The sorrel exploded under him, squalling with a mixture of fear and anger. Vince's right leg was in the air, swinging to pass over the cantle as the animal went into action. The horse lunged forward and pitched, and the cantle hit that right leg, knocking it back and turning Vince's body on the pivot of his left boot. He felt the boot slip on the step of the stirrup, then his left leg was driven through the stirrup up to his knee. His foot slammed against the street, and shock waves flowed up the leg and through his body, setting his teeth with the jar of them. He still held the reins in his left hand, and he hauled on them, trying to stop the sorrel's wild plunges.

The horse was fury released, and Vince was off

balance. It pitched again, jerking the reins from his hand and pounding that left boot against the ground. Vince's mouth flew open with the agony of it. His hat was snapped off, and his eyes blurred. He heard a distant yelling and was not able to tell the direction from which it came. Above the yelling was the drum of hoofs. That drumming could have come from the sorrel's hoofs, and the yelling was probably his own.

He fought to stay upright, knowing if he went down, the horse would kick and pound him to pieces in the street. The sorrel made another twisting, bucking lunge, and Vince's leg twisted under him, throwing him heavily to the street. The back of his head slammed into the ground, scattering his senses, and a black curtain moved in on him.

Through the haze of near unconsciousness he heard a woman's scream, and the pound of hoofs sounded nearer. The sorrel was still pitching and twisting, and Vince's leg had slipped out of the stirrup. But the foot was twisted at an awkward angle and caught. His body flopped and bounced with the sorrel's bucking, and twice a rear hoof came dangerously near his head. He threw his arms across his face, helpless now to stop the sorrel's lunging, or to raise himself. His body was bounced and dragged with every movement the sorrel made, and the blackness was much nearer. He had seen men thrown and caught in just such a predicament, and a hundred feet of such punishment was usually enough to drive the life out of a man's body.

His only hope was that some of the watching men

would spring forward and catch the sorrel's bridle and manhandle it to a stop. There was blood in his mouth, and his tongue felt as though he had bitten it through. The shirt was torn from his back, and with each convulsive pitch it felt as though steel claws raked his back and shoulders. He thought, dully, no one is going to do anything, and he welcomed the lingering blackness that would take him out of this endless pain.

He was dimly aware the sorrel had changes directions, that instead of bolting down the street it was heading for the buildings on the right hand side. He heard the slam of its hoofs on the wooden walk, felt the edge of it bite into his back, then scrape to his waist. He heard the woman's voice again, not screaming this time, but still loud and sharp with anger. It seemed to come from the other side of the sorrel, and he could not understand it. He heard the voice, imperative with its demand, order "Grab him, someone! You, Hoyt—Grab that horse!"

He could hold on no longer, and he let go, sliding down the long, black tunnel. It had a soothing warmth and release to it; it was so much better than all that pounding around out in the street.

4

HE CAME to, feeling someone fussing around his left knee. The street had grown suddenly soft, then he realized he was lying on a bed. He opened his eyes, and the pounding in his head made him instantly close them. A man's voice asked, "Feel it, eh?"

It held a tone of professional interest, and Vince opened his eyes again. He held them open despite the hammering in his skull and looked at the little bald headed man, fooling with his knee. He saw the black bag, sitting on the bed beside his leg and asked, "What have I got, Doc?"

"Enough," Doc Emeroy grunted. "A couple of thousand bruises and lacerations. But nothing is broken. You twisted this knee. Take care of it, and you may be walking before this week is out." He soberly regarded Vince. "You know how lucky you are, don't you?"

Vince raised himself on an elbow. He felt the clamoring protests of all those bruised places. His clothing had been removed, and he saw the raw, scraped places extended from his back to his sides.

The places had been covered with some kind of a soothing salve, and only when he moved did they cause him trouble. His face was clean, and the taste of blood and dust was gone from his mouth.

He asked, "Where am I?"

"Ron Goddard's house," Emeroy answered. He saw the puzzled look on Vince's face and said, "Hallie Goddard saved you. She was riding down the street just as that crazy horse of yours started to pitch. She hazed it up onto the walk. Before it could turn someone grabbed the bridle."

Vince remembered the woman's voice calling, "Grab him. You, Hoyt. Grab him." So he owed his life to Morgan. He did not give him full credit. Morgan had not made a move, until Hallie ordered him.

The picture of a long legged, awkward girl with pigtails and freckles flashed into his mind. Hallie Goddard. He had wanted to be around her often as a kid, but Morgan would not have it.

He said slowly, "I owe her something."

"Just your life," Emeroy said dryly. "Everyone else just stood around like they were spellbound." He snapped the bag shut and said, "I'll look in later on in the day."

Vince heard the firm, yet light beat of Hallie's footsteps coming toward the room. What did you say to a woman who had saved your life?

A tall girl came through the doorway, and his tongue was frozen. The pigtails were gone. Her hair was a luxuriant, auburn mass, piled high on her head. In the dim light of this room he was not certain of the color of her eyes. They could be green, or a gray-green. He suspected they would change shades with her moods. The rough man's shirt she wore could not hide the youthful curves. Her cheekbones were too high, too wide, her mouth too long and full for real beauty; but there was a force, an attractiveness about her that pulled a man's attention. She gravely looked at him, then smiled—and he saw he was wrong about her not being a real beauty. His heart was thudding faster than usual, and his throat and mouth had an unusual dryness. He knew how he used to feel about her, when he was a kid. It looked as though that was one thing that had not changed.

"She asked, "How do you feel, Vince?"

"All right." How he felt was not the important subject.

"Hallie, Emeroy told me what you did. I won't attempt to say my thanks. You must have had me brought here."

She said scornfully, "Where else could you have gone? The hotel? You needed attention."

Her eyes were brilliantly hard because of some thought. She said, "Dobie must be afraid of you, or of the reason you came back. He hasn't forgotten anything. He wanted to see you dragged to death."

He shook his head. "He didn't have anything to do with it. The sorrel is only half broken. I should have been more careful with him."

She shook her head in disagreement. "I was close enough to see it all. He waited until you started to swing up, then swept his hat in front of the horse's nose. Maybe he couldn't figure on it turning out the way it did, but the least he expected was to see you thrown."

A voice drawled from the doorway, "You've got to excuse Hallie. She's got an imagination."

Vince looked toward the door. He had not heard Hoyt Morgan come in. By Hallie's start, neither had she.

Morgan leaned against the door-jamb, an odd little smile on his lips. The smile held no warmth, and it did not lessen the probing hardness of his eyes.

He said softly, "Hallie is noted for picking up all the stray dogs and cats in town. Looks like she's at it again."

Hallie's eyes were furious. "Hoyt Morgan, don't you know enough to knock?"

The rebuke bounced off Morgan. "The front door was open. I didn't have to knock. You trying to hide something, Hallie?"

His eyes sharpened at the increased color in her face. "You pick up another stray dog, Hallie?" he murmured.

She walked to him, and Vince noticed she was as tall as Morgan. "Why were you just standing around? Why did you let someone else stop that horse? And why did your boss spook him in the first place?"

So Morgan had not grabbed the sorrel after Hallie's order. Vince said, "It looks like I was giving you undue credit, Hoyt."

Morgan's eyes were hardening, and there was an ugly set to his jaw. "I didn't come here for anything from you. Hallie lets her imagination run away with her. Dobie had nothing to do with that horse spooking. He just took off his hat. Can you find a law against that?"

"I see," Vince said. He did. Hallie was right. Her imagination was not involved at all. But proving the accusation was another matter. "You tell Dobie he'll never lay a hand on that horse. And if he comes around me again, I'll break his damned neck."

Morgan's neck was turning as red as the wattles of a turkey cock. Before he could speak, Hallie said scornfully, "Tell Vince the real reason you came here, Hoyt. Tell him I went with you a few times, and you got the idea you owned me. Tell him I ordered you to stay away after you went to work for Dobie."

That was madness filling Morgan's eyes. "Hallie, I'm warning you—"

Vince propped himself up in bed. He did not notice the half hundred stabs it caused him. "Don't say anything you can't back up, Hoyt."

Morgan threw an oath at him. "I'll back up anything I say."

Vince started to throw the sheet from him, and Hallie checked him with a gesture of her hand. "You'd better get out of here, Hoyt, before Ron comes in. He doesn't have much use for you, anyway."

Vince saw a man crazy with rage. Morgan was half crouched, leaning toward him. Vince knew a jab of worry. Morgan was armed. His own gunbelt hung over the back of a chair, some five feet away. He could not get close to that gun, if Morgan moved.

Morgan fought some inner fight, then said thickly, "I'll be seeing you again, Vince." He whirled and stomped out of the house."

Vince lay back and let a long sigh escape him. He felt that had been close. Morgan had teetered on the edge of a decision. He could have just as easily fallen the other way. Vince knew one thing for certain. All strings of the past association between them were broken. It still brought its little mournful sense of loss.

Hallie was looking at him, her head half cocked to one side.

"Vince, did you come back looking for Dobie?"

He shook his head.

"But he thinks you did?"

"I don't know what he thinks." He watched his fingers picking at the sheet. After their meeting in the saloon, Hoyt had run to Dobie as fast as he could. He remembered Hoyt's questions about the old homestead.

She leaned forward and placed an anxious hand on the back of one of his. "Vince, you'll be careful."

He placed his other hand on top of hers. He saw the lovely color suffusing her face. "Hallie," he said softly. "I sure will."

She jumped at the sound of a footstep and jerked her hand free. Vince mentally cursed as Ron Goddard came into the room. The past moment could have been built into something. He knew it.

Goddard's eyes did not miss the confusion in her face. "What's going on here?" he growled.

To cover that confusion, she said, "Hoyt was just here."

That was plain mad in Goddard's eyes. "Why?" he demanded. "I thought you told him to stay away."

"You know I did. He came to see what Vince was doing here."

Goddard took in the apparent damage to Vince's hide. "Not so well, I'd say." He half grinned at his frosty assay at humor. "I heard about you being throwed. You all right?"

"Emeroy says nothing broken. Hallie had me brought here."

"Where else would you go?" Goddard growled.

Vince relaxed. For Goddard, that was holding a door wide open.

Goddard sat down on the gunbelt-draped chair. The gun butt gouged him, and he impatiently shoved it aside.

"Hallie says Dobie spooked my horse."

"Did he?" Goddard demanded.

Vince shrugged. "That sorrel's only half broke. Anything can start him." He looked at the indignation in Hallie's eyes. "Maybe Dobie did."

Goddard's eyes were probing again. "And that gives you an excuse to go after him?"

Vince said wearily, "I didn't come back to dig up the past. I don't want the old homestead. I heard Maw blame Dobie a thousand times for what happened." The old guilt was back in his eyes. "He was only a name to me, Ron. I never could hate him like Maw did."

Goddard grunted, "I'm glad to hear that. But Dobie won't believe it. And by the look on Hallie's face, when I came in, I'd say Hoyt is plenty riled. He won't believe you either."

Goddard's face was gloomy as he stared at the far wall. "Maybe the reason you came back is worse. Another wild horse hunter."

He made it sound like horse thief, and Vince reared up. His voice was heated. "What's wrong with that? What's wrong with—"

Goddard interrupted him. "The last two groups who outfitted from here didn't come back. One group was found lying around a dead campfire. Most of them had been shot while they were sleeping."

Vince weighed Goddard's words. "What happened to the other group?"

"They were never found."

He saw the look on Vince's face and said angrily, "It's a big country. A posse could search for a month and never find a track. Those horses probably wound up across the border. I know one thing for sure. If you're smart, you won't go after horses from here. If you're half smart you won't tell anybody you're going after them."

He started for the door, and Vince asked, "Ron, who's behind it?"

The hot glare faded from Goddard's eyes, and an additional stoop seemed to be in his shoulders. "I've got an idea," he said in a weary voice. "For ten years,

I've been waiting for him to make a mis-step. Ten years of watching him grow fat like a hog and not being able to stop it."

"Dobie Nerich," Vince said flatly.

"Dobie Nerich," Goddard repeated, and the savagery was back in his voice. "Don't you think I knew your mother was right, when she came to me? And I couldn't do a damned thing about it. Proof! I had to have proof. I still need it. I see him laughing at me, every time he passes me on the street. He picks up these harebrained kids like Hoyt Morgan. Kids, who never had anything. He waves some easy money in front of their faces, and they listen to him. Dobie Nerich is behind every crooked dollar around here. I know it, and I can't do a thing about it." He advanced a couple of steps toward Vince and stabbed a finger at his face. "This doesn't mean you've got leave to go after him. The law protects him just as much as it does anyone else. When you bring me proof, I'll nail him."

"Did he kill those hunters?"

"I think he did. What could be an easier way to pick up a good piece of money than by letting someone else do the work of gathering a band of horses, then stepping in and taking them away?"

"And you think he'll come after me, when he knows why I'm here?"

"He'll come after you," Goddard said grimly.

"Then I'll stop him." Vince made it a flat, positive statement.

Goddard walked to the door and turned. "That will be a different matter then. You can protect yourself. You're welcome to stay as long as you like."

"Thanks," Vince said. But the door was already closed.

Hallie said, "It worries him, what happened to those hunters. And now to find out you're one—" She shook her head and did not finish.

Vince grinned. "He's not that worried over me."

"No, over Colin. Colin wanted to go with the last bunch of hunters. When he learns you're going, he will be impossible to hold this time."

He recalled Colin as a nuisance of a kid, always tagging along where he was not wanted. That was a long time ago, he thought. Colin would be about eighteen now.

"Colin thinks he's grown up. He talks all the time about the money and fun there is in hunting wild horses."

"Some money and fun there is in hunting wild horses."

"Some money, Hallie," Vince said. "And some fun. But mostly it's hard work. I don't intend to stay in it all my life. After I get a stake—" He was suddenly aware of the way his tongue was running away with him. He was used to the lonely spots where a man conversed inwardly with himself. And now he was putting all those thoughts into words. He admitted the thoughts had a new trend to them, with a vague purpose at the end of the trend. It happened the moment she walked into the room.

Their eyes locked, and she said unsteadily. "You call, if there's anything I can do for you."

He stared at the ceiling, after she was gone. He had a drum in his chest, and each beat shook his body. It made a man nervous and mighty glad to be alive. He said, "You go slow, boy. You go mighty slow until she gets used to seeing you around."

A smile spread across his face. Now what legitimate excuse could he use to call her back into the room? He was still trying to fashion one, when he fell asleep.

5

WHEN HER knock on the door awakened him, the sun's slanting rays told him it was afternoon.

He assured her he was all right, and she said, "A Captain Simas is here. He wants to know if you feel like talking to him."

Vince raised himself, ignoring the sharp jolt of pain. "You send him in here right away," he said eagerly.

Simas came into the room, followed by a hulking trooper. The sergeant's stripes were as faded as the material of his shirt.

Simas held out his hand and grinned. "Is that bed what you're going to ride to catch those horses for me?"

Vince returned the pressure of the handclasp. Simas was a short, square man with a rough-hewn face. His bearing and manner were all Army, but Vince liked him. He had liked him when he first met him in Santa Fe.

"Maybe that's the safest four-legged thing he can ride," the trooper grunted.

He towered over Simas by a good six inches. He had a jaw chiseled out of granite and remote, hard eyes. His contempt for anyone outside of the Army was plainly apparent.

Simas laughed at Vince's angry coloring. "Vince, this is Sergeant Brady. He thinks only the Army can do anything right."

Vince looked at Simas and said, "So you heard about it?" He was not even tempted to explain. Explanations would be a sign of weakness, and he doubted Brady would believe, or even listen.

"I heard he dumped you. Goddard showed him to me at the stable. That's a lot of horse, Vince."

"If the Army buys him, see that he's given to Sergeant Brady, will you?"

Brady colored at the implication. "I can ride him," he growled.

Simas chuckled. "That's enough from you two. Vince, I'm authorized to buy a hundred horses, if they're anywhere near as good as the sorrel. At a hundred dollars apiece."

Vince drew a deep breath. A hundred horses at a hundred dollars a head . . . That was ten thousand dollars. With that sum of money, a man could make plans for the future—plans that could include anyone he wanted.

Simas' eyes were probing. "Can you supply them?"

Vince had no idea where he could find a hundred wild horses anywhere near the quality of the sorrel. He said in a voice not quite steady, "I can supply them."

"Within thirty days?"

The time limit made it rough. But who could expect an easy path to that kind of money? "Within thirty days," he said.

"Good," Simas said briskly. "I'll expect to pick them up then. I'll have a detail here on the twenty-fourth of next month."

"They'll be ready," Vince said. They would be, even if he had to scour all of New Mexico and throw in Arizona.

Morgan found Nerich in the back room of The Black Butte Saloon. "That Army officer went to see Vince," he reported.

Nerich's eyes gleamed. "Now what business could the Army be having with Carwin?"

Morgan shook his head. "The Captain went to the hotel. The Sergeant's at the Eagle's Nest."

"Drinking?"

"Like he's trying to put out a fire."

Nerich heaved himself to his feet. "We'll join the Sergeant. A thirsty man always loves company. Particularly when the company does a little buying.

He walked down the street, Morgan at his heels. He liked it that way. Besides, the walk was too narrow for both of them to comfortably walk side by side.

He stopped inside the entrance of the saloon, and he did not need the uniform to pick out the hardest drinking man in the room.

Nerich moved to the table and asked, "May I buy a drink for the Army, Sergeant?"

Brady's glass was empty. Why not let a damned civilian buy the Army a drink? Or as many as he could get.

He waved a hand at the empty chairs. "Sit down," he mumbled. His eyes gleamed as Nerich ordered a bottle and glasses to the table.

Nerich talked of inconsequential things until the level of the bottle was considerably lowered. Then he casually asked, "Just passing through town, Sergeant?"

Brady had trouble in focusing on him. "Business," he mumbled. He leaned toward Nerich. "Did you see that sorrel?"

Nerich gravely nodded. "A lot of horse, Sergeant."

"Too damned much horse for the man who says he owns him." He leered at Nerich. "I'll bet he stole him. Hell! He can't even ride him."

Nerich nodded. "You may be absolutely right, Sergeant. Is your business with him?"

"The Captain thinks it is. A hundred dollars," Brady said thickly. He belligerently locked eyes with Nerich. "And don't tell me that horse isn't worth it."

Nerich nodded and got to his feet. "He's worth all of that. It's been nice talking to you, Sergeant."

Nerich did not speak again until they were a dozen strides from the saloon. "A bottle of whisky for that information, Hoyt. A bottle well spent."

Morgan had been doing some figuring. "Dobie, that comes to—"

"I know what it comes to," Nerich interrupted.

"Ten thousand dollars—a nice, tidy sum. We'll keep an eye on Mr. Carwin. We'll let him do all the work of gathering them. Then we'll step in and help him. We'll collect the money for them." He felt in a wonderful humor. He always did, when someone else was doing the work for him.

Hallie came into the room and said, "Vince, will you talk to him? I can't keep him out any longer."

"Who?"

"Colin. He's been pestering me all afternoon to let him talk to you."

Vince grinned. "Let him in, Hallie."

Colin Goddard bounded through the doorway. He must have been listening outside it. There was little resemblance between him and Ron Goddard. His color must have come from his mother's side of the family. He was lanky and tow headed; a man in height, needing only filling-out in a few places, but still a kid in enthusiasm. His eyes had an intense shine, and Vince saw a lot of Hallie in them.

Colin said, "Vince, I heard what you're after. I want to go with you. I don't give a damn about the pay."

Vince shook his head. "I am looking for hands, Colin. But they've got to have experience." Simas gave him thirty days. It was not a lot of time in which to make his gather and break the animals."

"Experience!" Colin yelled. "I've chased wild horses. I've caught a few and brought them back."

"Were they any good?"

Colin colored. "Maybe not like that sorrel of

36

yours," he muttered. "But you didn't start on something like that."

He had a point there. Vince saw a kindred feeling in Colin Goddard, a love of horses and a need to chase the wild ones. He sympathized with him, but he could do no more.

"No go, kid," he said. "Ron would skin me, if I told him you could go along. And I'm not bucking him."

Colin swore and stormed out of the room. Vince thought, They'd better take the reins off him. He'll be going on his own anyway.

He looked at Hallie and ruefully smiled, "I've made someone else unhappy with me."

She callously shrugged. "He'll get over it."

He grinned as she left the room. Big sisters never had much room for sympathy with a kid brother's wants.

Despite the doctor's warning, he tried the leg the following morning. He could not lay around in bed for a week as Emeroy wanted. That would be too big a bite out of his thirty days. There was still some swelling in the leg, and he winced as he bore his weight on it, but he could hobble around after a fashion. Hallie watched him, displeasure on her face. "You're hard-headed enough to go ahead despite what anybody tells you."

"I've got to, Hallie. I've got to get some things done."

She sniffed and lifted her sewing, but he noticed she covertly watched him. He had found her in the front room, working on the voluminous folds of material in her lap. She looked clever with a needle, and the dress was nearing completion. The soft green of it would go perfectly with the color of her hair.

He asked, "Special occasion coming up?"

Now she seemed determined not to look at him. She bit off a piece of thread and was very much occupied in poking it through the eye of the needle. "A dance tomorrow night."

He gave her a puzzled frown. What was he supposed to say now?"

While he was trying to choose something, she gave him an angry flash of her eyes. "You might ask me to go. Why do you think I picked this spot to sew on this dress? So you would see it."

That charged current was coursing through him again. "It was in my mind to ask you," he said. "But I won't be able to do much dancing. I didn't think you'd want to go with me."

She said tartly, "Don't you think I should have the choice of deciding?"

He moved to her and placed his fingers on her arm. "Hallie." It was trouble keeping his voice even. "Will you go with me to the dance?"

He saw the radiant shine in her eyes and the flutter of pulse in her throat. "Oh yes," she said softly.

It was a moment that could have been richly developed, but Goddard and Colin came in then. Vince thought woefully, A man should never get interested in a girl who had a family.

Goddard looked at Hallie, and the radiant shine

was still in her eyes. "What did you swallow that makes you look so pleased?" he growled.

He sounded tough with both Hallie and Colin, but few widowers could have done a better job in raising children.

She said, "Vince is taking me to the dance tomorrow night."

Goddard looked from her to Vince, then back at her again. "With Hoyt still in town. You really like to stir things up, don't you?"

She had a temper, and it flared. "Am I supposed to sit around doing nothing, just because Hoyt is in town?"

Goddard glared at Vince. "Do you know what she's leading you into?" His voice took on a bitter edge. "The one thing I ask for is peace. And that's the one thing I don't get. I've got a feeling you're piling a heap of trouble on this house." He turned and walked heavily out of the room.

Hallie's temper was still unexpended, and it had to come out on someone. She looked at Vince. "If what he said worries you, you don't have to take me."

He smiled at her, trying to restore her good humor. "I'm not backing out now," he drawled.

"Backing out," she said furiously. "That's a nice way to put it." She stormed out of the room.

Vince glanced at Colin. "What did I say wrong?"

"How the hell do I know?" Colin said. "You wouldn't back me up. You could've talked him into it, if you'd wanted to." He reached the door in three long strides and slammed it behind him.

Vince sighed as he sat down. He swore softly. He had the whole family down on him, and he had hardly opened his mouth.

6

HER SPITEFUL humor carried over into the next morning. She rebuffed every attempt he made to talk to her. And if he said dance—that was like lighting a dynamite fuse. "We're not going," she snapped. "I wouldn't want you to get into any trouble."

Her perverseness made him want to shake her. Instead, he turned and left the house. He limped downtown and bought a new shirt and a pair of trousers. It was a nice piece of material in the shirt, and its color would go well with her dress.

He came back, and she was dusting furniture in the front room. He opened his sacks and said, "I bought these especially for tonight. And I'm not intending to waste any money on them." He seized her shoulders. "We're going to that dance."

Her red hair was still in the ascendency. "We are not! Who do you think you are to tell me—"

She was looking up into his face, and he quickly bent his head and kissed her. She was stiff with either surprise or resentment; then he felt a quiver run through her. He drew her close, and the pressure of his lips increased. He knew the exact moment of her capitulation, for a melting seemed to go all through her. She thew her arms about his neck, and the eagerness of her lips matched that of his.

She said his name over and over, and the trembling in her body grew. He thought, soberly. This is no new thing. It's old. It's always been there, waiting for us to find it.

"Vince," she said, her cheek against his. "I was afraid after what Ron said you wouldn't want to go. I was afraid you'd think I was playing you and Hoyt against each other."

He held her at arms' length. "I believed what you said about Hoyt," he said simply.

She briefly shut her eyes, and when she opened them, they were suspiciously bright. She came to him again; then broke away. "I've got a thousand things to do before tonight, and you're mixing me up." She evaded his hands and left him.

How's Goddard going to take this? he thought. Not well, he knew.

Vince shined his best pair of boots and was dissatisfied with the results. He shined them again, and he put a mirror surface on them. He looked at himself in the glass. He thought he would do. He saw the excitement in his eyes. Hallie, Hallie. As long as that name remained in his mind, he would never be lonely again.

He sucked in his breath when he saw her. The dress was a perfect compliment to her hair, and its color picked up the shining lights in her eyes. Her shoulders were bare and softly rounded. She did not have to ask him if he liked the dress. It was written all over his face.

Goddard looked at them, and a heavy sadness was in his eyes. "It was bound to happen," he said flatly. "Don't you think I could see how things were shaping up?" He shook his head at Vince's expression, and his voice softened. "I put no blame on you. I'd think you were crazy if you didn't know she was around. But one thing builds another, and I'm just thinking of what this could be building. Watch yourself, Vince."

Vince soberly nodded and led her outside. They had received a blessing from Ron Goddard, even though it was a left handed kind of blessing.

People were converging on the schoolhouse ahead of them, and he heard the scraping of a fiddle. The excitement made him light-footed. Who needed the ground to walk on? He said, "Hallie, I'm going to try a dance. I'll make this leg stand up for that much."

She laughed up at him; then the laughter abruptly faded. A man stepped out onto the walk from the shadow of a bush and blocked their way.

"I was coming for you, Hallie," Morgan said. His eyes burned into Vince. "I'll take her the rest of the way."

Hallie half gasped, then she cried, "Hoyt Morgan, are you completely crazy?"

Vince looked at the jealousy-wracked face. Hallie's question was pretty near right. He said,

"Stay away from her, Hoyt."

Morgan's flash of teeth looked like an animal's snarl. "Or what?"

"Or I'll make you."

Morgan crouched. "Maybe you'd better start now."

Vince felt the slam of worry. He was unarmed. Morgan was wearing a gun. But surely Morgan would not be foolish enough to use it with all these people around. But a jealous mind might not even see those people.

Vince pushed Hallie from him. He and Morgan were about six feet apart. If he could get a good push off his uninjured leg, he might be able to cover that distance before Morgan drew that gun. He knew he was kidding himself.

"Hoyt!" a voice called from off to the right. It called the name a second time before Morgan heard it, or Vince recognized it. Dobie Nerich was calling Hoyt.

"Damn you, Hoyt," Nerich said. "Get over here."

Morgan looked at him, then back at Vince. "I'll see you again."

"Any time," Vince said— The hollow inside him was slowly filling with relief. He would be sure the next time he saw Morgan he would be wearing a gun. Those people might not have existed to Morgan, but they did to Nerich. Nerich was not going to see one of his men get himself hanged by gunning down an unarmed man. Vince's lips moved in a mirthless smile. He guessed he owed Dobie

Nerich a little something.

He took Hallie's arm, and he could feel the trembling in her. Near tears showed in her voice. "He's crazy, Vince. And I'm scared."

Her fear was for him, and he tried to soothe her. "Nothing is going to happen, Hallie. Hoyt will cool down." He remembered the maniacal glare in Morgan's eyes. Morgan was past the stage of cooling down.

Nerich jerked Morgan into the shadows. His belly shook with his rage. He started to cuff Morgan across the face; then thought better of it. "You damned fool," he said. "You crazy, damned fool. If you gunned him, Goddard would have you on the end of a rope before the night was out."

Morgan said savagely, "Nobody walks in and takes away my girl. Nobody."

Nerich swore at him. He used every vile name at his command. "She never was your girl. You stood around like a moonstruck calf, waiting for her to come to you. You never get a woman that way. You walk up and take her. Your chance at that is gone. You'd have to kill Carwin now—"

"I'll do that."

Nerich grabbed him by the shoulder. "You try something like that, and I'll kill you. Do you understand me, Hoyt? I'll kill you. He's going to put together the biggest piece of easy money we've had a crack at for a long time. And you're talking about killing him."

His fingers dug deeply into Morgan's shoulders.

Morgan shivered. Not at the pressure of the fingers, but at the savage intensity in the eyes. He was not afraid of Vince Carwin. But he was afraid of Dobie Nerich. He could not say what the difference was.

"I'll wait," he muttered. "But it better hadn't be too long."

Vince danced the first dance with her. The rest of him might respond to the excitement; the leg did not. He was stiff-legged and awkward. A girl like her deserved more than this. He said, "You find yourself another partner. I'll just look on."

A man claimed her, and Vince settled down on a bench along the wall. He felt no jealousy watching her dancing with another man. She would be thinking about him. Something in the way her eyes warmed after he released her told him he was wise. The chain wasn't made that could bind a person, if she didn't want to be bound. You tied a person to you with the soft ropes of tenderness and understanding.

Morgan came into the building after the third dance and caught Hallie as she was leaving the floor. He held out his arms, and Hallie shook her head. It was an emphatic gesture, denying him the next dance and a thousand after it.

Morgan turned his head and gave Vince a long, malevolent stare. A man got the same kind of appraisal from a coiled rattlesnake.

Near the end of a late dance, a man touched Vince on the shoulder and said, "Goddard is outside. He wants to talk to you."

It was odd that Goddard should send for him like this. Then he remembered Goddard's vague displeasure with him. Something had happened to increase that displeasure, and Goddard did not want to jump him before all these outside.

He said, "All right," and followed the man outside. He did not try to tell Hallie. He would be back before the present dance was over.

The man said, "He's over here." He led the way across the street, and Vince limped after him.

Morgan stepped out of the shadows, leaving someone behind him. Vince did not know him. It was not Nerich. The bulk was not big enough.

He recognized the set-up as soon as he saw it. He had three of them against him. He said evenly, "Hoyt, I'm not trying to push any trouble. Why don't you let it alone?"

Morgan's anger made him almost inarticulate. "You're getting out of town. Tonight."

He swung a fist, and Vince blocked it with his left forearm. The second blow slipped through, crashing into his mouth. The power of it put a roaring in his head. He rocked back from Morgan, put a hand to his cut lips, then said coldly, "You shaped it this way, Hoyt."

He was in an awkward position, hampered by a stiff leg and unfavorable odds. Morgan did not bring the other two along to see Hoyt Morgan take a beating. Vince had one thing in his favor: Morgan's blind anger. If he could keep his head and let Morgan's blindness make the mistakes . . . He used his good leg in slipping aside from Morgan's rush. As Morgan went by, Vince drove a fist into Morgan's belly. It was a good blow—Morgan's momentum increasing its force—and Vince knew savage satisfaction as it pulled a deep grunt out of him.

He gave ground, buying time with his retreat. Morgan kept making those furious rushes, trying to overwhelm him with brute power alone. Vince's fists cut and slashed, draining away a little of that enraged strength with each blow. Every time he used the injured leg, it gave him a hard twinge. It was still better than getting his head knocked off.

Morgan stopped and panted, "Stand still, you son-of-a-bitch."

His face was a pale blur in the semi-darkness, and Vince heard the rasp of his breathing. A man could recklessly burn up his strength and spend it in a few furious moments, or he could spread it out to cover the situation. Vince decided Morgan had saved but little. He pushed off the good leg, getting leverage behind the blow. He sledged Morgan full in the mouth, and Morgan reeled backwards, spitting blood and curses. Vince did not give him time to recover. He rained in blows, and each fist was a sharp edge chipping away an additional bit of strength. He was hit in return, but Morgan's fists were losing their kick. He slugged Morgan in the face, and Morgan clawed open handed at him. The fingers of a hand closed on his shirt, and the front of it went with the raking grab.

Vince hit him again, and he was punching at an almost defenseless man. Morgan sobbed for breath, and his weary arms kept sagging on him. He stumbled under a punishing blow to the belly and somehow remained on his feet. He reeled and staggered, his hands pawing blindly before him.

"You can call it off now, Hoyt," Vince said. "Or I'll finish it."

He was seized from behind and the surprise of it momentarily choked off his breathing. He struggled in the grip of the two men. In the heat of the fight, he had forgotten all about them. One of them had a grip on his right arm, hammerlocking the hand up toward Vince's shoulder blades. His chin was pressed against Vince's neck, and Vince felt the scrape of his beard stubble. He threw his body about in a threshing arc, and his imprisoned hand was jerked higher. The pain of it stopped his struggle.

They forced him back against a building, and one of them said, "Here he is, Hoyt. Take him."

Morgan's breathing was jerky and labored. He weaved as he studied Vince. His blood-smeared mouth was thinned to a cruel line, and his eyes were wild with hate. Vince saw the blow coming and tried to pull his head aside. The fist slammed into his cheekbone. The agony threatened to tear off the top of his head. Morgan's face faded into a foggy blur. He took three more punches in rapid succession, each of them knocking his head back into the wall. He lashed out with his boots, whipping his body around, trying to throw off the men holding him, and each time Morgan waited until they had him upright again. The savage fist would land, jolting an additional bit of Vince's senses away. The roar in his head was magnifying. A great sullen cloud of blackness hovered at the rim of his consciousness, and he wanted it to move in and blot out this torture.

He heard a voice, and it seemed to come from a thousand miles away. He heard it again, and this time he could make out the words. "That'll be enough of that," the voice yelled. "I said hold it."

The hands pinioning Vince dropped away, and he staggered and almost went down. He leaned against the wall, head hanging on his chest, trying desperately to hold onto his fading senses.

Morgan said, "Stay out of this, kid."

"You try to put me out," the voice said and went into a string of oaths describing Morgan and the two other men.

Vince lifted his head. The pounding in it lessened until it was only a dull hammering at the base of his skull. He saw Morgan glaring at Colin, saw the other two warily watching the kid. Colin held a pistol in his hand, and his face worked with anger.

Colin said, "A fair fight's one thing. But what you were doing—" His mouth twisted, and Vince thought he would pull the trigger. Morgan thought so too, for his face grew alarmed. He retreated a step, holding out his hand. "Now wait a minute—" he started.

Vince said huskily. "Thanks, Colin." He took a forward step, forcing the protesting leg to bear his weight. He took another one, pivoted on it, and slammed Morgan in the side of the face. His hurt

50

and anger were behind the blow, giving it an awesome force. It knocked Morgan across the walk and into the street, and his feet went out from under him.

A hand seized his arm, half pulling him around. "That's enough," Hallie said. "That's more than enough."

He looked at her, and tears were streaking her face. Tears for him, he knew. He had not seen nor heard her come up. Most of the people in town seemed to have been drawn to the scene, and he looked at them with dull eyes.

He said, "Sure, Hallie." He was glad for her supporting arm.

Colin said excitedly, "After Vince whipped him, those two grabbed him. Morgan was knocking his head off, when I stopped him."

Hallie said incredulously, "Hoyt was hitting Vince, while those two held him?"

Colin vigorously nodded.

Morgan was getting to his feet. His eyes were still vacant and his mouth was slack. Hallie's voice was vibrant with anger. No one, anywhere near here, would have any difficulty in hearing her.

"You're an animal," she said. "Don't you ever dare try to speak to me again."

The passionate loathing in her voice reached even Morgan's dulled senses. It was an ugly face that looked at her. The face turned slowly toward Colin, then to Vince. He had never seen such hating in a man's eyes. Hallie had called Morgan down before all these people, and he would never forget or forgive her for that.

Hallie took Vince's arm. "Come on now. I want to fix your face."

Vince was wise enough not to attempt to grin. His face would not stand it. It felt as though it could stand a great deal of fixing.

7

HALLIE FINISHED doctoring his face, moved back a couple of steps, and inspected her work. He could tell by her expression that he looked like hell. He was stiff and sore all over and now his face hurt. He thought with wry humor, Another day or two in this town will kill me.

He tried to make a joke of it. "Maybe you should have taken Hoyt. He couldn't possibly look this bad."

She said fiercely, "Don't joke about it, Vince. Didn't you see the look on his face. He looked like a crazy man."

He thought soberly, She was right. Hoyt did look crazy. And the looking usually preceded some kind of action. Out there in the street, after he had been beaten, when the townspeople saw him beaten, when Hallie called him an animal, Hoyt had stepped over the edge. He would not attempt to climb back to sanity; he would only wait for a better time and circumstance to wipe out the source of his hating.

Vince's expression as he thought about it was too grave, for Hallie saw it and shivered. "Vince, I'm frightened."

He held out his arms and said, "Come here." Her fright was for him, not herself. Arms could soothe away fears better than any words could.

She started to move toward him, and Goddard came into the room. Vince thought sourly, Goddard had a knack of bad timing.

Goddard scowled at him. "You keep pushing it along, don't you?"

Hallie's eyes flamed. "Hoyt started it. He tricked Vince into coming outside; then the three of them jumped him."

Vince chuckled. The three of them did not jump him. Two of them only held him.

"Stop it, Hallie." Goddard's voice was tired. "I know what happened. I asked around about it. Hoyt got everything he asked for. But now, Colin's been pulled into it. Hoyt isn't a forgiving man." He popped a knuckle and was unaware of the action or sound. "Colin pulled a gun on him and ordered him around. You think he will forget this? I just brought Colin home with me. He thinks he's all growed-up now. I had to hear a dozen times just what he done. I wanted to knock the strut out of his voice."

Vince said quietly, "He saved me a bad beating, Ron." Maybe more.

Goddard said testily, "I know, I know. But do you know what Hoyt is going to do? He'll wait until the time is right. Then he'll back Colin into a wall. There won't be anyone around to help Colin. Hoyt will cut him down just like that." He made a snapping sound with a finger and thumb. "And it'll be legal because Colin will try to fight him. He's a big, growed-up man now, and nobody can call him out."

Hallie made a little, moaning sound, and Goddard flashed at her an angry glance. His anger was not really directed at her but at his helplessness.

Vince said, "Ron, maybe it would be best to get him out of town for awhile. It would give Hoyt a chance to cool down. I could take Colin with me."

He thought Goddard was going to explode.

Hallie said warningly, "Paw," and Goddard made a choking sound.

He glared at Vince. "After I've told him a half hundred times he couldn't go?"

"He'll be easier to keep an eye on out there than here in town." It would also keep a brash, young kid from further affronting Morgan.

Goddard realized it, for a weary expression was settling over his face. He turned his head and yelled, "Colin!"

Colin must have been listening right outside the door, for he threw it open before the sound of his name faded.

"Yes," he said eagerly.

Goddard frowned at him. "You're going with Vince. I've got a job to do. I can't watch you every minute. And I can't watch every alley and street in this town." His expression grew more fierce. "You're under Vince's orders. You do everything he tells you to and do it right. If you don't, he's got my permission to take the hide off you."

Colin's yell of exuberance shook the house, and Vince hid a covert grin.

Vince slept late the following morning. The sharp pains of his hurts were gone, but the stiffness was worse. He dressed and limped out into the kitchen. Hallie smiled at him, but there was concern back of the smile.

He guessed at her thoughts. Now two of the men she loved were involved in this.

He shook his head at her concern and said softly, "It's going to be fine, Hallie."

She came to Vince, and her arms went about him. He held her close, feeling the vibrant softness of her. She said, "You'll be careful?"

He put a finger under her chin, lifting it. "I'll watch out for Colin," he promised. Her mask of indifference could not hide the concern she felt for her brother.

"You watch out for yourself," she said fiercely and kissed him long and hard.

He found Goddard at his office. The windows looked as though they had not been washed in a dozen years, and the interior was as bad. Goddard sat behind the battered old desk, his face brooding.

"Don't you ever clean this place out?" Vince asked.

"Had it cleaned last year," Goddard growled. He was in no mood for idle banter. "Morgan's still in town. He must have been drinking all night. I could throw him in jail, but that won't solve a thing. He'll only wait until he gets out." He shook his head and said gloomily, "I'm in a bind, Vince. If Colin stays around town, Morgan will jump him. If he goes with you, I don't know what will happen." He lifted his head, and his eyes were piercing sharp. "Watch him close, Vince. Watch every step he makes. Don't let that fool kid out of your sight."

"We can watch him better out there than around here."

The words carried no reassurance for Goddard. He was thinking of two bands of horse hunters, two bands that did not come back.

"Maybe," he muttered. He shoved a piece of paper across the desk top toward Vince. "Here's a list of men I'll personally vouch for. Hire any or all of them. And get out of town as quick as you can."

Vince stuck the list of names in his pocket and nodded. "As fast as I can," he promised. He would hate to leave Hallie. But the quicker he left, the quicker he could return.

His last arrangement was made by the evening of the second day. He hired eight men, paying them the going wage of forty dollars a month. But he promised them a bonus of ten percent of the total sale to be split among them. That would come to better than a hundred dollars a man. It added to a tidy sum; it would help insure loyalty, and it should certainly make for added effort. Those men would want that bonus as fast as they could get it.

He was satisfied with the men he hired. They

looked as though they came out of the same mold—
lean, hard-bitten men with remote eyes and an inner core of restlessness that made them jump at his
offer. He hired the two Clayton brothers and Dan
Abel. He hired Stu Hall and Hobe Driscoe. One
man went only by the name of Whit, and if he
wanted to keep a lid on his past, it was all right with
Vince. Tom Austin was older than the rest, and his
age might be a steadying influence on the others.
Jose Mendoza was the last man he selected. Mendoza was strongly recommended by Goddard as a
man who knew every foot of the wild horse country.
He was swarthy and short with coarse, black hair,
showing his Indian and Mexican strain. His teeth
were startlingly white against his dark face, and
they flashed often in wide smiles. He spoke fluent
Mexican and the dialect of a half dozen Indian
tribes. He would have double usefulness—as a
tracker and as an interpreter with the wandering
Indian bands they might encounter, particularly the
Navajos.

Vince had eight competent, reckless horsemen,
and it would take both traits to make this hunt a
success. He trusted them because Goddard said it
was safe to trust them.

He bought a wagon and a team to pull it. He
stocked the wagon with provisions for ten men for
thirty days. He bought a dozen spare mounts, personally inspecting each one, grunting his approval
if the animal was sound. After a couple of sly at-
tempts to include a wind-broken animal and a tired,
aged horse, the horse trader showed Vince only his
best.

"He said, "You bought some good ones.""

Vince nodded. He needed good ones. Those horses had hard running ahead of them.

It was after dark when he walked into the Goddard's kitchen.

Hallie said crossly, "I've tried to keep your dinner warm in the oven. Don't blame me, if it's burned."

He watched her as he ate. Something had sure happened to upset her.

He said, "It's good, Hallie." He supposed it was.

Her distant expression did not change. "I'm surprised you found time to notice it."

He knew then the basis of her displeasure with him. He had given her too little time, and she was hurt and resentful. He saw her for a few brief moments in the morning, and even then he was too engrossed with his plans to do much more than say hello. It was the same at evening.

He said, "Hallie, I've been busy. You know that. I've had a thousand things to see to."

"You weren't too busy to talk to Colin last night," she snapped.

He had talked wild horses to Colin for an hour last night. But that was different, and a woman should understand that. He grinned and asked, "You jealous of your brother?"

That put flaming color in her face and sparks in her eyes. "I'm not jealous of anything you do," she said crisply. "You can get that through your head right now."

He put his feet under him and approached her. "Yes, you are," he said. "And you stay that way."

He seized her wrist. "Come outside. I've got something to say to you."

He pulled her across the kitchen floor, and she resisted every step of the way. He got her outside and wrapped both arms about her. She still struggled. She tried to stomp his feet; she tried to butt him with her head.

"You going to fight all night long, Hallie?" he asked plaintively. "How can a man ask a girl to marry him, when she won't stand still long enough to listen?"

He heard her gasp; then she was suddenly limp in his arms. He gently shook her and asked, "Don't you think you ought to answer me one way or the other?"

She pressed her face close against his chest, and he was sure she was crying. "Oh, Vince," she said in a muffled voice. "I've been awful. But I've never been in love before. And it hurts. I thought you were just amusing yourself until you found something more interesting to do."

He lifted her face and kissed her. Her lips trembled under his and carried a salty taste. He said, "You're not very bright, Hallie. But I think you're going to learn real good. Why do you think I've been so busy? So I can get away, finish my business, and come back to you. If I'm lucky, Hallie, I can ask you to marry me and not be ashamed of the asking."

She pulled his head down to her level and kissed him. Her lips were firm and demanding this time. "Now who's talking foolish?" she asked.

He said gravely, "I'm almost broke, Hallie. No man likes to come to a woman that way. This last hunt will let me settle down. Settle down the way I want for both of us. It's only for a month, Hallie. You'll wait that long?"

"Longer than that, Vince. Much longer than that."

An orange moon rode high in a cloudless sky, and the stars were close enough to reach up, pick one out, and hand it to her. It was a rare, perfect night, the kind of a night a man should pick to make his proposal.

"Do you feel like walking?" she asked.

He could walk a million miles as long as she was beside him.

He said, "We're going into the Alta Mesa country, Hallie. It's big plateau country—a favorite range of wild horses. The Army wants a hundred horses, if I can gather them quick. I've hired good men. Ron recommended every one of them. There's a horse out there I've never seen, but I've heard about him. They call him El Caballo Padre. It means the father of horses. We'd call it great horse. He's supposed to have collected the finest bunch of mares in the country. I want El Caballo Padre and his mares. If I bring enough of them back, the Army will pay me ten thousand dollars."

He heard her suck in her breath and laughed. "I felt the same way, when I first heard that amount. Now you know why this hunt is so important to me."

8

THE TEN riders, the extra horses, the wagon and team made quite a cavalcade leaving town the following morning. Vince had hoped to leave earlier, but a half hundred irritating delays seemed determined to stop him. When they were finally in motion, he looked back at Hallie and Ron Goddard. He lifted his hand in a salute, seeing the gravity in both their faces. They would worry until the moment this string of riders headed back into town.

Colin swept off his hat and waved it in the general direction of his sister and father, at the same time raking his horse with his spurs. The horse made vigorous protests with a half dozen lunging bucks, and Colin's shrill, excited yelling filled the air.

It was kid stuff, and it made Vince partially angry. Here those two were worrying over him, and Colin was showing off. I'll take it out of him, he thought. I'll chore him to death at the evening's camp. He looked at Colin's shining eyes in a happy face and could not stay angry. Let him have these bright happy moments. They went so damned fast; then the kid was gone, and a man was left.

He lifted the reins and moved down the street. He looked back and the string of men and horses followed him. He had twenty-seven days to catch a hundred wild horses. It would not be a day too many.

As he passed the Eagle's Nest Saloon he saw Dobie Nerich and Morgan standing before it. He was sorry Nerich knew of this hunt, but there was no way of keeping an operation of this size a secret. If Goddard was right in assuming Nerich was behind what happened to the other horse hunters, then Vince would hear from him again. The thought clamped the iron hand of worry on him. The responsibility of Colin's safety was a big burden. But there were ten of them, and it would take a large force to successfully jump a camp that was alert.

Morgan would not look at him. His eyes were fastened on Colin, and Vince was close enough to see their savagery.

Colin never lost his enthusiasm during the day's ride. He was up and down the string of riders, talking to first one, then another. They pumped him full of ridiculous stories, and he accepted them as gospel. He rode most with Jose Mendoza. And Mendoza talked freely with him, his white teeth flashing often.

When they made camp, Vince judged close to twenty miles were behind them. Whit did the cooking, and Colin willingly helped him. He gathered mesquite wood for the fire, he ladled out portions and poured the coffee. He was the butt of rough humor, and he accepted it with a grin. He was going to be a favorite with these men before the hunt was over.

Vince finished his supper and idly listened to the talk about him. This was big, silent, brooding country. Somewhere in the distance a coyote yapped disconsolately, waited for an answer, then yapped again. A man could think that only himself and the coyote filled that emptiness. But he could not rest too securely on that assumption. For a cavalry troop could be bivouacked a mile or two from him, and he would never know it. Or it could be Dobie Nerich, Vince thought soberly.

He assigned the night watches before he turned in. Colin wanted one of them, and Vince refused. He took the edge off his refusal by saying, "Later, Colin. You'll be standing your watch like the rest of us." But right now he wanted experience and an older, more alert mind keeping watch.

Colin was not ready to go to sleep. "Vince," he asked, "is it true about this Caballo Padre? They've told me so many things I don't know what to believe."

He wasn't as much kid as they thought. He was beginning to try and sort things. "I've heard about him," Vince said. "I've never seen him."

"Jose claims he saw him less than a month ago. He couldn't get close enough to lay a rope on him."

Vince nodded. "It could have been Caballo Padre. I'm relying on Jose finding him for me."

"You won't settle for anything else?"

"I'll settle for anything I can find. But most

bands of wild horses are small. Stallions are jealous
of the mares with them. Let another stallion try to
approach, and you have the damndest fight a man
ever saw. I've seen two of them. The way they bat-
ter and tear each other to pieces will scare you. But
now and then several bands will seem to agree to
throw in together. The reports say Caballo Padre is
heading such a bunch. That's why I'm hoping we'll
find him."

Colin said, "I'd like to be the first one to see
him."

That would be important to a kid, and Colin
might go to any lengths to accomplish it, even to
going off on his own. Vince said sharply, "You get
that idea out of your head right now." He wanted
Colin in sight of one of them at all times.

Colin's face fell. "I thought it would be different
out here."

If he expected to find no discipline, he was
wrong. The country itself imposed a rigorous code
of action; the actual gather would bring a different
kind.

"You'll do nothing on your own," Vince said.
"You understand?"

He watched Colin make up his bed. He might
have put it easier to him. But he thought irritably,
there's no time to put it easier. Colin would have to
fit the unit, not the unit him.

They were riding an hour after dawn. If last
night's rebuke subdued Colin, it did not show. He
was up and down the line, asking his innumerable

questions. He was a good kid, Vince thought with sudden affection. Rash and brash, but that was a kid's prerogative.

Mendoza joined Vince just before noon. "Water ahead," he said. "Not good water, but it will do for the horses. We may find some sign around it."

Mendoza was right about the sign. Vince could see the hoof prints twenty yards away.

"How many, Jose?" he asked.

Mendoza hunkered down, studying the tracks. He turned his head and said, "twelve. Not more than fifteen. Two or three days ago."

"Is it Caballo Padre?" Colin asked.

Mendoza laughed. "You expect me to tell from a hoof print? But I would say no. He would not have such a small bunch." He smiled at the disappointment in Colin's eyes. "Maybe tomorrow. Maybe the next day we see him." He straightened and said, "But now we will use this water."

Vince was idly sweeping the country with his eyes. No instinct alerted him, and he expected to see nothing in this emptiness. His eyes started to move from a dark butte rising to his left, then came back. For an instant, he thought he saw a flash of light—a flash such as the sun might make striking a pair of field glasses.

"Jose." His tone alerted Mendoza. He followed the direction of Vince's gaze and was silent for a long moment.

"I see nothing," he finally said.

"Maybe I imagined it," Vince muttered. "But I thought I saw a gleam of light."

Mendoza continued staring, then shrugged. The gesture was all things—an acceptance, a denial. But his words were all acceptance. "We will have to keep the closer watch at all times."

They nooned at the water hole and moved on through the hot afternoon. They saw their first band just before dark, a small, fairly nondescript group consisting of a stallion, a dozen mares, and four or five yearlings.

Colin wanted to break down into the little valley after them, and Mendoza shook his head. "It is a small bunch. Not worth the while."

Vince agreed. "From here, that stallion isn't much. If the stallion is poor, the quality of the mares won't be any better."

Mendoza nodded. "An ugly, misshapen man cannot expect to have his pick of the beautiful women. So it is with the animals. After tomorrow's ride, you can begin looking for the great horse."

While they watched, the stallion threw up its head and tested the breeze. It stood in tense immobility for a long moment, then whinnied shrilly and whirled. Its hoofs drummed against the earth, and the sound carried faintly to the motionless men. The stallion broke into full flight, and the mares followed him. Vince watched them race away, tails and manes streaming. The stallion had caught something alien in the breeze, or an uneasy instinct had warned him.

Vince looked at the rapt expression on Colin's face. That one was born to be a wild horse hunter.

By the evening of the third day, they were well

inside the Alta Mesa. Vince had a good feeling about this hunt. There was harmony among the men, and the hunt could not help but be successful — if they were left alone.

He finished his third cup of coffee and sighed with repletion. Mendoza had found sign and said it could have been made by Caballo Padre's bunch. Tomorrow could be an exciting day.

He looked at Colin across the campfire. The kid was pumping Mendoza for all he was worth, drawing out every last detail. Vince grinned at Mendoza's patience. Colin was horse-crazy.

The blackness cloaked them, and the solitude of the little group seemed complete. The breeze stirred the sand with a faint, slithering sound, and he heard the hunting cry of a coyote. Some nocturnal bird made a swishing sound as it swooped at something. But there was no tearing, agonized cry. Evidently it had missed its prey. The hunting coyote and the hunting bird belonged in this land. Everything was at its appointed task, and he could find no discordant note. Yet something would not let him fully settle down. It could be the persistence with which he remembered that flash of light, or it could only be man's natural tendency to borrow trouble when there was none in sight. He saw the dark, moving silhouette of Stu Hall as he paced near the picketed remuda.

He considered irritably, At least no surprise will overrun us. His precautions were probably being taken a little early. If someone was watching them, they would not move now. They would not move until after the gather. They would let all the work be done, then try to scoop up the spoils.

He thought, The responsibility for Colin's safety is too great; it's too much of a load. Vince knew the weight of that responsibility prompted part of his curt words to Colin; his weariness made up the rest of it. In the morning, he would make up to Colin for his harshness.

He finally dropped off into uneasy sleep. He did not know how long he slept, but the night had the feeling of being late. The air was thin and cold, and the stars were paling. He looked to the east, and the first false light of dawn was a thin, sullen gray streak on the horizon. He looked across to where Colin slept, and he saw no softly blurred mound. He stared, telling himself he was imagining things. Colin's blankets were there, but they were flat against the earth.

He crawled out of his blankets and pulled on his boots, flogging his sleep-heavy mind to remember who had the guard watches. Colin was not one of the men he had assigned. Hobe Driscoe was supposed to have the last tour.

He moved to where Driscoe slept and stirred him awake with a boot toe. Driscoe blinked, trying to focus his eyes, and Vince said, "I thought you were on watch."

Driscoe sat up and yawned. "I was ready to relieve Austin, when the kid said he'd take it for me. He said he couldn't sleep anyway." He came wide awake at the expression on Vince's face. "Did it make a difference?"

"No difference," Vince said. He would make nothing out of it until he was sure. He understood how a sleep-craving man would jump at Colin's offer.

He walked to the picket line, and the horses snorted and stamped at his approach. He spoke softly, quieting them, and moved along the line. Colin was not in sight. And his horse was missing.

His face worked with wrath. Colin had ridden off someplace and left a sleeping camp unguarded. No excuse could justify that. If Colin thought Vince was harsh last night, he would remake his opinion after Vince got through with him this morning. Vince intended stripping the hide off him.

He moved back to where Mendoza was sleeping. He touched him, and Mendoza awakened like an Indian, instantly and completely. Vince squatted down beside him and asked, "What were you and Colin talking about last night, when I told him to put out the fire?"

"Caballo Padre," Mendoza answered. "I told him we were near the great horse, that his favorite watering place was not more than a dozen miles away."

Vince swore explosively, and Mendoza watched him with concern. "I did wrong. Yes?"

"Not you," Vince said savagely. "That damned kid. He's gone. He's riding right now toward that water hole. He wants to be the first to spot the stallion, then come back and tell us." He could guess at the workings of Colin's mind. Colin was going to prove something to himself, to all of them.

Even if Colin found the stallion and his bunch, he could spook the entire band, making them that much more difficult to find and handle.

"We're going after him," Vince said. Uneasiness was prodding him. He had promised Hallie and Goddard to keep an eye on Colin every minute. That promise was shattered. He swore again. From now on, he would not let Colin get a rope's length from him.

9

Colin looked back, and Driscoe was already crawling into his blankets. He was trembling with excitement. He would come back and announce that he had spotted Caballo Padre. Or he would be first on the scene, triumphantly pointing out the wild bunch, when Vince arrived. He had the directions to the water hole thoroughly in mind, and he wanted to leave now. He looked back at the sleeping men. If he left camp unguarded now, Vince would blast him, but he could leave a half hour or so before dawn. The little time remaining until light could not possibly make a difference. He picked up his rifle and moved toward the picket line.

It was still dark when he saddled and led his horse away from camp. But dawn could not be too far away. He moved some five hundred yards before he thought it safe to mount. The sound of hoof beats, even in sand, could carry. He did not want Vince awakening and stopping him. He turned in a southwest direction, scoffing at the thought of getting lost.

The sun came, and the first touch of it was welcome after the chill of the night. The wind was rising with the sun, stirring the sand ahead of him. If it strengthened too much, it would become a broom sweeping all tracks before it. After he found the wild horses it might be better to keep an eye on them. He nodded in sudden decision. That could save Vince two or three days in hunting them. That should please him. The ground rose, and the horse's hoofs rang against an outcropping of rocks. He thought he must have covered at least half the distance.

He swung around a bald knob, and his heart rose and lodged in his throat. Hoyt Morgan sat a horse before him, and evil grin on his face.

Colin's hand made an abrupt move, and Morgan said, "Go ahead. Give me an excuse."

Colin looked at the pistol in Morgan's hand and dropped his arm to his side. He was frightened. His heart was pumping at a fearful rate. He tried to keep his face blank as he asked, "What do you want?"

"You don't sound friendly at all," Morgan said. The grin did not leave his face. "And here I've been sitting waiting for you all this time. I saw you coming a long way off. You wouldn't want me just riding off and leaving you."

Colin tried to put bravado in his voice. "I'm on an errand for Vince. He'll be sore as hell if you stop me."

Morgan's face turned raw and violent. He cursed Colin, and he cursed Vince. Colin realized that

Vince's name was a match to the fuse of Morgan's anger. Morgan finally got control of himself and said, "Dump your guns. Just make one wrong move. Just look like you're thinking about it."

His savage expression begged for Colin to be foolish. Fear was crawling over Colin with slimy feet. He thought, Why, he's crazy. He carefully picked his pistol out of its holster and let it drop. He drew the rifle from its scabbard and let go of it. He felt naked and very lonely.

"Move," Morgan said, waving his pistol toward the southeast.

"Where are you taking me?"

"Don't ask any Goddamned questions!" Morgan shouted. You just move in the direction I tell you. Don't open your mouth again, or I'll beat it closed."

Colin knew numbing fear as he rode. Vince, he kept thinking. The name repeated itself in his mind like a little prayer. Why hadn't he listened to Vince? But he had wanted to prove so many things to him. Now if Vince did not find him . . . He's got to find me, he thought frantically. He told himself that Vince and Mendoza were already tracking him. He wanted to twist his head about to see if he could spot them and dared not. Morgan was in a dangerous temper. The slightest move could shove him over the edge into raw violence. Colin kept switching his eyes. Morgan could not see that. But Colin could not see very much in the limited radius of the swing of his eyes. And, too, the wind was carrying sand with it, stinging his face and forcing him to close his eyes. Behind him, he heard Morgan swearing at the wind.

Colin judged they had ridden some five miles when they came in sight of the camp. He saw the heavy bulk of a man ponderously raise himself and come forward. He was too far away to clearly see the features, but that bulk had to be Dobie Nerich. No one else around was that large. He knew a vast relief. Dobie would calm this crazy Morgan. Dobie had nothing against him.

He saw the harsh working of anger on Dobie's face as they rode into camp. He quickly counted. Dobie had fourteen men, counting Morgan. It was a big force, and he wondered why they were here. He did not like the way their eyes bored into him. There was too much hunger in them, too much expectancy.

Dobie yelled, "I sent you out to keep an eye on them. And you bring him back here. Of all the damned fool tricks!"

For a moment, Morgan seemed to ignore him. "Get down," he ordered Colin. He emphasized the command with a thrust of the pistol's muzzle.

For an instant, Colin thought his legs would not support him. His fear had hollowed him, leaving only a thin, unreliable shell.

He said, "Dobie, Hoyt's acting crazy." He tried to work indignation into his tone. "What right did he have to stop me and bring me here?"

Morgan swung down and moved to within a stride of him. "You'll get your reasons," he said softly, and it carried more menace than if he had shouted it.

He looked at Dobie and answered his question. ".I was riding out to keep an eye on them. Like you told me. I saw him coming and waited. He was headed in this direction. I was afraid he would stumble onto us."

"He's a liar," Colin shouted. "I wasn't coming in this direction at all."

Morgan's fist slammed into the side of his face. He was not braced for it, and the force and unexpectedness of it sent him sprawling. He looked up from the sand and his head was ringing; his eyes refused to focus.

"You like to call me a liar again?" Morgan asked.

Someone laughed, and it had a far-away sound. Colin shook his head to clear it and half raised himself. His arms tried to refuse his weight.

Nerich asked, "Why did you bring him, Hoyt?"

"Like I told you," Morgan said, his tone protesting any other purpose. "Suppose he'd spotted us and gotten away. You want that?"

Nerich shook his head. No, he did not want that. He suspected Morgan was lying, but he was helpless in the bind of circumstances. He scowled at Colin and said, "We can't turn him loose now."

"I didn't intend to." Morgan reached down, grabbed a fistful of Colin's shirt, and hauled him to his feet. "He's a smart, big man with a gun in his fist. He showed off before a lot of people in town. I want to see him show off again. He's got people watching again."

He slammed his fist into Colin's mouth, letting go of him at the same time. The blow knocked Colin down; it put an additional sickness into him. A gagging sourness was in his mouth, and there

seemed to be at least three Hoyt Morgans weaving
back and forth before him.

Morgan strode to him and kicked him in the side.
The brutal force of it jolted Colin a foot along the
sand. "Get up, you son-of-a-bitch," Morgan said.
"I'm going to beat your head off."

Colin heard whoops and laughter. Somebody
said, "Show us a real fancy job, Hoyt."

Nerich put piercing eyes on Morgan. So that was
it. Morgan had brought Colin here for personal re-
venge and no other reason. He wanted to beat him
to a pulp before watching eyes. It would achieve a
measure of satisfaction for the queer twist in
Morgan's mind. Nerich had no intent of stopping it,
now that it was started. It was entertainment for the
camp; it would fill a few minutes for bored, half
quarrelsome men. But this was the second time
Morgan had disobeyed him. His usefulness was
running thin.

Colin crawled toward Morgan. He seized him
around the knees and painfully tried to draw himself erect. If he could only clear his head, if the
damned top of his skull would stay in place instead
of threatening to fly off. . . He wanted to fight this
dirty bastard. He wanted to hurt him, at least just a
little in return for the hurt he had suffered.

Morgan let him raise his head above his waist,
then threw a brutal elbow into his face. It jolted
Colin's hold loose. He sank to his knees, then slowly
sagged forward. Morgan brought up a knee, catching him full in the face. His face was a bloody
wreck, the features blotted by the rushing blood.

He went over backwards, landing heavily on his shoulders. He was still not out. He tried to roll over, to get his hands and knees under him. He half made it, then fell forward on his face with a tired sigh.

"You didn't let it last long enough, Hoyt," one of the men complained.

Morgan threw him an unseeing look. His chest was heaving and the wildness distorted his face. He wished that had been Vince Carwin, and—yes—Hallie.

Nerich said, "You've had your fun. Now get rid of him. And dump him far enough away from us so it won't cause any trouble. If Carwin tracks you here, I'll tear you to pieces."

Some of the wildness was leaving Morgan's face. "Track me in this wind?" he scoffed. "This wind won't leave a sign."

He drew his pistol and aimed it at the back of the unconscious head. He held it aimed a long moment, saving the moment. He enjoyed this. And there was more enjoyment ahead. This was just partial repayment. To collect the bill in full, he would have to deal with Carwin and Hallie.

He pulled the trigger, and Colin's head jerked. He fired twice more, though he knew it was not necessary. He scowled at the body. Now he had to cart it away. He decided he had better take it back toward the north.

"Take him a long way," Nerich said. "You'd better be damned sure Carwin doesn't come storming in on us." The warning in his voice was plain.

10

MENDOZA STARED into the distance. He shivered as though a cold wind touched him and said, "I have a bad feeling about this."

Vince did not belittle the words. That was Mendoza's Indian blood talking, and so much Indian blood had a strain of the mystic.

They pushed the horses hard in reaching the water hole. Both of them yelled and fired their rifles, and there was no answering call nor shot from Colin. Worry was eating deeply into Vince now. He asked, "Jose, is he lost?"

Mendoza shrugged, and it had a fatalistic quality. "I only hope it is no worse," he said.

Vince's face was tight as he stared about the country. A man could get lost in it so easily. He accepted the fact that Colin was lost because it was the least of the ugly things that could have happened.

Colin was not at the camp when they returned, and the fact made Vince sick in his stomach, sicker than he ever was from a horse's kick.

He saw the worry in those still faces as he talked to the men. In a short time, the kid had made himself popular and liked. He said, "Fan out in all directions. If any of you find anything, fire three shots. Try to be back here by dark."

They nodded and moved to their horses. Many a swear word would be spent on Colin, when he was found, because of this moment of anxiety.

Vince rode to the southeast. To his right and left he occasionally saw the moving dots of Dan Abel and Bill Clayton, almost out of range of the eye. He kept listening for the report of a rifle; he kept hoping he would find some reason to fire those shots himself.

He returned to camp just as it was getting dark. Mendoza and Hall were already there, and they gave him negative shakes of their heads. The others trickled in at short intervals, and each had the same negative gesture.

The evening meal was a silent one. They ate out of habit rather than wanting. They sat in a quiet ring, each man occupied with his own thoughts. Somewhere out there was a lonely, frightened kid.

"We'd better find him by tomorrow evening," Driscoe muttered. "Or it won't be much use in looking any longer."

The others gave him baleful looks for putting into words what was in their own minds.

Vince slept poorly that night, and he suspected the others did the same. He was awake an hour before dawn, and he cursed its slowness in coming.

Driscoe found Colin by mid-morning. Vince

spurred toward the faint sound of the rifle shots, his heart sick with dread. Four faint dots circled over-head in the distance, dots that gave Vince basis for his dread.

Driscoe was squatting a dozen yards from the body, his face turned from it, when Vince arrived.

"They led me here," Driscoe said, looking at the circling buzzards. "They were a lot lower, when I arrived."

Vince put a glance on the great birds. The eaters of carrion, the markers of death. They were coward-ly birds, circling for two or three days until they were certain no movement could come from the ob-ject below. He did not have to ask about Colin. The buzzards told him.

He started toward him, and Driscoe warned, "He isn't pretty."

Colin lay on his back in the sand, his face horribly beaten.

"He's been shot in the back of the head," Driscoe said. "At least a couple of times. It was probably done after he was beaten unconscious."

Vince's cursing was no release for the helpless rage he knew.

Others were coming, drawn by Driscoe's shots, and each man went through the same procedure. First, the shock on their faces at their first look at Colin, then the rage, followed by helpless swearing. Mendoza squatted beside him for a long time. He straightened and said, "He knew so little time," and it was a protest against the waste of it.

He cast about in ever growing circles, and the

men silently watched him. He came back to Vince and said, "I do not think it happened here. I think he was brought and dropped here. The sand beneath him is pressed down hard. But with the wind—" His shrug said, Who knows where to start looking?

Hall said, "We're gaining nothing by standing around here. Let's get after him."

"Who?" Vince asked. "And where?"

Hall said explosively, "It had to be Morgan. Who else hated him this much?"

Vince nodded agreement. He, too, thought it was Morgan. He asked, "Where do we start looking, Stu?"

Mendoza muttered, "They're out there. Someplace. But a man could hunt for weeks for them."

"Good God!" Hall yelled. "We're not just going to let this pass by."

"No," Vince said. "We're not letting it go. But the quickest way to bring them to us is to finish the hunt. If they're here for the reason I think they are, they'll come to us."

He saw argument on some faces, and others were nodding in agreement with him. He said crisply, "Go back to camp and wait until I return. I've got to take Colin home."

"I would like to ride with you," Mendoza said.

Vince gave him a grateful glance.

They took Colin back to camp and lashed him to a pack animal. Vince mounted and looked down at the hard, watching faces. "Keep a sharp eye," he said. "We'll be back as soon as we can."

He made the pace as fast as the pack horse could stand. He pushed hard the rest of the day and deep into the night. They were moving again at the first light of the following day. He and Mendoza talked but little. Once Mendoza said, "He was filled with laughter. And there is not enough of that."

It was after dark when they arrived in town. Goddard's office showed no light, and Vince muttered, "I was hoping he would be here." He looked at Mendoza and said, "I guess we'll have to take him home."

"Si," Mendoza said.

Vince left the pack horse in the shadows of a bush and walked reluctantly toward Goddard's door. He would never do a harder thing than what was ahead of him.

He knocked on the door and heard the light footsteps coming toward it. He thought. Not Hallie. Don't let her answer.

Hallie opened the door, and the sight of Vince put a quick anxiety in her face, for he should not be here now.

He said, "Hallie, I've got to see Ron."

She clutched his arm, and he could feel her trembling in her fingers. "What happened, Vince? Is it Colin?"

She read the confirmation in his eyes, for her face went white and stricken. She whispered, "No," as though there were no greater sound in her, and he saw the sobs shaking her shoulders. The sobbing was soundless and the more terrible for the lack of it.

He seized her shoulders, knowing the sickness of helplessness. No one could do anything for her at the moment. He said, "Hallie, Hallie," and took her in his arms. He doubted she heard his words, nor felt his touch.

He lifted his head at the sound of heavy footsteps crossing the floor. Goddard's voice demanded, "What is it?"

Goddard's face changed as he saw the sobs shaking Hallie. He looked at Vince's bleak face and said in a lifeless voice, "Colin?"

Vince nodded. He knew there were no easy words with which to tell them. Hadn't he searched for them for hours? He said, "Everyone tried to watch him. But he slipped out of camp. He was wild to be the first one to spot the big horse."

For a terrible instant, Goddard's eyes blazed at Vince, filled with accusation. Then the blaze died, and his voice was dead. "I guess no one could have stopped it. I guess I knew it was going to happen from the moment I heard Colin pulled a gun on Morgan. Maybe I was the one who failed. I should have killed Hoyt there and then."

Just as Vince had, Goddard took it for granted that Morgan was the killer. His face sagged, and he looked twenty years older as he asked, "You couldn't find any sign of him?"

Vince shook his head. "We had a strong wind after Colin left. It broomed everything clean. Mendoza was helpless."

"No proof again," Goddard muttered. "We know, but we can't prove it. A coroner's verdict will

say he was killed by a person or persons unknown."
He was talking to himself, thinking like a lawman.

Vince said savagely, "He's out there, and I know
it. Maybe you can't act, but I can. Do you think lack
of proof is going to stop me?"

Hallie looked at him with tear-swollen eyes. "Kill
him, Vince." Her tone was contained, at odd vari-
ance with her grief-ridden face—and the more demanding because of it.

"I will, Hallie," he said. He looked at Goddard
and said, "Ron, if you'll come with me now . . ."

Hallie started to follow, and Vince shook his
head. "No," he said flatly. "There's nothing you
can do."

When the door closed behind them, he said, "He
was badly beaten, Ron. Then shot in the back of the
head. I didn't want her to see him now."

Goddard stared at his dead son, his face a harsh,
inscrutable mask. His voice had a lost, lonely quality as he said, "I was thinking of all the times I gave
him hell."

Vince nodded. He knew how Goddard felt. The
last words he had spoken to Colin had been on the
harsh side. No amount of self-torture would undo
them. He knew that, too.

He touched Goddard's arm and said, "Hadn't we
better take him to Packley's?" Packley was the town
barber and undertaker.

Goddard gave a long, heavy sigh. "I guess we'd
better."

Vince led the pack horse, and Goddard plodded
along beside him. He said, "I'm going back with

you." He looked at Vince, twisted hating in his face. "Did you think I was quitting because I had no proof?"

Vince said, "I'm glad, Ron. I think we'll have to bring them to us. A successful gather will do that."

Goddard nodded. "I'll bury Colin in the morning; then we'll ride."

Mendoza came out of the shadows as they reached Packley's. "I have awakened him," he said. "He is waiting for you." He looked long at Goddard. "I am sorry, Senor Goddard. I would have liked to have ridden with your son for many days."

Goddard briefly clasped his shoulder. "Thanks," he grunted. He strode into Packley's, and Vince let him go alone, thinking Goddard would be better off that way.

He was finishing his cigarette, when Goddard came back. Goddard moved to the pack animal and began untying knots.

Vince started forward, and Mendoza seized his arm. "If he needs the help, he will ask for it," he said softly.

Goddard untied the body and lifted Colin in his arms. He walked through the door. His step was burdened, but his head was high.

"I almost feel sorry for this Morgan," Mendoza said. "The list of people, wanting to kill him, is getting longer."

Vince thought of Hallie; he thought of Goddard seeing Colin under a light. "He'll get it," he said grimly.

"That is for sure," Mendoza said softly.

Goddard returned and said, "Obe will fix him up. We'll bury him at nine o'clock in the morning."

It was an early hour but best. The sooner it was over, the sooner Hallie and Goddard could begin their recovery.

Goddard said, "You two come on home with me. There's plenty of room to throw a pallet on the floor."

Mendoza murmured, "Gracias. But I am used to sleeping under the sky. A house closes me in."

"I'd better stay with Jose," Vince said.

Goddard nodded and plodded heavily in the direction of his house.

Mendoza said, "A stranger cannot share sorrow."

Vince was not a stranger to the Goddards, but he knew what Mendoza meant.

Vince was relieved when Colin's funeral was over. He stood beside Hallie at the grave, her quiet sobbing tearing him to shreds. Goddard stared blank-faced at nothing. The final prayer was said, and Vince took Hallie's arm and led her away. He turned his head and said sharply, "We're losing time, Ron. We'd better be moving."

Goddard broke his trancelike stare and followed them without argument. Vince half expected one. But it would have done neither of them any good to watch the filling of the grave.

Goddard said, "I got to stop at Mayor Ortman's house. Hallie, you go to your aunt's. Stay there until we get back." He walked on ahead, giving Hallie and Vince a moment alone.

It was bad leaving her this soon after her loss, but it could not be helped. He said, "You take care of yourself. I'll bring Ron back as soon as I can."

She clung to him for a moment. "Bring both of you back. I could not stand it, if you did not." She kissed him, then gave him a little push. "I want you to go."

He looked at her wan attempt at a smile, touched her cheek, and walked away. He did not look back.

Goddard joined Vince and Mendoza at the livery stable. His badge was missing. Vince looked at the holes in the vest the pin made. It was odd to see Goddard without that badge.

"I turned it in," Goddard said gruffly. "I wanted a free hand. It gave me no jurisdiction out there, anyway. Ortman said I had to put it back on, when I returned."

"He is going back with us?" Mendoza asked, and his eyes were bright.

"You got any objections?" Goddard grunted.

"I am for it. But I did not expect you to leave—"

"My town?" Goddard finished the sentence for him. "Maybe that's going to surprise a lot of people."

He swung into the saddle and moved down the street, looking neither to the right nor left. This was no longer his town, and he was not concerned with what it did.

Mendoza shook his head. "A hard man," he said. "An unknowing eye would say he has no room for grief. But he is filled with it. And it will make him even harder."

11

GODDARD YELLED against the shouted arguments, "And I'm telling you the quickest way to get them is to find those horses—"

Vince's men were not happy with Goddard's words. They had listened to Vince talk, they could identify the men out there watching them, and here Goddard was saying they should go ahead as usual.

Dan Abel said, "He was your son. I don't see how—" He fell silent under Goddard's piercing eyes.

The fury in Goddard's voice was poorly contained. "Don't you think I want them bad? Don't you think if I knew where they were that I'd go after them? Tell me where they are. Which direction do we ride? Do we go in a bunch? We can't split up. It'd be too dangerous. If we stay in a bunch, it'll take weeks to search even a little part of this country. We know they're watching us. They'd merely move ahead of us. Give me some answers. I'll listen."

Driscoe said sullenly, "It's galling to just go ahead. But maybe it's best."

His words ended the argument. None of them were happy about it, but they accepted it.

They spent the next three days hunting horse and saw another small band. Mendoza kept saying, "The big herd should be around here someplace." He shook his head in perplexity. "But not even a sign have we found. I do not like the looks of it, Amigo. Has he a place I do not know about? Or has something frightened Caballo Padre? Has he moved his band out of the country?"

That gnawed at Vince, too. The passing days were biting into his allotted time.

Mendoza said, "A countryman lives in the next valley. Roque Ceron runs sheep there. Maybe he had seen or heard reports of the great stallion."

Vince said wearily, "Anything is worth trying. Can we reach it by night?" At Mendoza's nod, he said, "We'll camp there."

Ceron's home was an adobe house in a fertile, watered spot, making a green oasis in the surrounding brownness. No one was in sight as the riders approached. Mendoza rode on Vince's left, frowning at the quietness. "This is wrong," he said. "They should be here. It is not the shearing time. What could have called them away?"

Vince watched the house. The quietness was not normal. Lonely, isolated families, such as this one, welcomed visitors. There should have been barking dogs, children dancing up and down, women peering cautiously from windows or doorways, and the men of the family coming forward, their faces beaming at the opportunity for talk with new faces.

They were two hundred yards from the house, when the nasty, whining crack of a rifle sounded. Vince heard Goddard cry out, saw him reel in the saddle and grab desperately for the horn. He kicked his horse toward Goddard's animal, yelling, "Hang on. Hang on."

He grabbed Goddard's reins and whirled the animal, spurring hard away from this spot. He caught distorted glimpses of the rest of his men, racing away in a scattering fan, bending low over their mounts' necks.

He halted out of rifle range and helped Goddard out of the saddle. Goddard leaned heavily on him, and his face was gray and screwed tight with pain. Vince's hands were bloodied after helping Goddard to the ground. He thought of Hallie, and he wanted to yell his fear. Not her father, too! Not coming immediately upon the heels of Colin's death.

12

THE SUN was halved by the western horizon, when an outrider turned his horse and spurred back to Nerich.

"House up ahead, Dobie," he said. "I didn't go too close."

"See anyone?" Nerich asked.

The man shook his head. "I thought I heard sheep. It's probably one of those sheepherder outfits."

Nerich pondered, then made a decision. "If someone built a house there, then there should be good water nearby. God knows we need some. The scum we've been drinking is eating holes in my belly. We'll camp there tonight."

Morgan overheard him and said, "Is that wise, Dobie? Carwin's behind us. King's last report said he was heading in this direction."

"He won't get this far tonight," Nerich said.

Morgan shook his head. At times, Dobie was awful thick. "If we camp up ahead tonight, and Carwin comes along this way, those people are going to talk about us."

Nerich scowled at him. "What are they going to tell him? Our names? What we're doing here? Maybe you're going to give them all the information they need."

A red wave washed Morgan's neck, and he said sullenly, "You've been so damned secret. Now, you're going in where people can see you."

Nerich leaned over and stabbed a finger at his face. "You tore the secrecy all to hell, when you killed the Goddard kid. Do you think Carwin believes the kid fell and hurt himself? I'll bet right now Vince Carwin's got your name in his head. Goddard's out here for the same reason. That's how much secrecy you've got left."

Everytime he thought about it, anger at Morgan almost choked him. He had not foreseen that Carwin would find Colin's body and take it back to town. He had not foreseen that Goddard would return with him. It meant that he had to be damned sure that everyone in that horse camp was killed. It was his original intention, but Morgan's action had put pressure on him.

He controlled his anger and said abruptly, "We'll camp up ahead, like I said. Goddamn it!" he said explosively, "I'm tired of looking at your faces. I want to see a new face. Even if it's a Mex sheepherder."

He was tired of looking at these bearded, sullen faces. Maybe Morgan was right about the danger of staying here, but probably he could fix it so that the Mex would not give his whereabouts away. And there might be women on this property . . .

"Hoyt, I've seen some damned good looking Mexican women in my time." A hot and lusty feeling stirred in his loins. He wanted a woman—any kind of a woman. He licked his lips and said, "She wouldn't have to be so damned good looking tonight."

Morgan's face remained indifferent, and Nerich swore at him. There was only one woman for Morgan, and Nerich knew her name was constantly on his mind, for too many times he had caught Morgan staring moon-eyed across the desert.

He said, with a testy laugh, "You're never going to get her, Hoyt. Because you don't know how to handle a woman. You're eating your heart up, waiting for her to come to you. When we get back, I'll show you how it's done. I'll break Hallie in for you."

Morgan turned wild eyes on him. "Goddamn you, Dobie!" he exploded. "Don't you ever say anything like that again."

Nerich said evenly, "I was only funning you, Hoyt."

His words did not appease the wildness in Morgan's eyes. Morgan jerked on the reins and his horse fell back from beside Nerich. Nerich did not turn his head to follow him. His eyes looked reptilian in a cold face. Morgan did not know it, but he had outlived his usefulness. He was never coming out of this desert. After the horses were taken from Carwin . . . Nerich toyed with the thought a moment, then let it go. He did not know what would happen to Morgan, or just how, but it was going to happen. He would let time and circumstance shape it for him.

Hallie stuck in his mind, and he licked his lips. He had been funning Morgan, but now the joking was all gone. Why not? She was a damned good looking woman, and Goddard and Carwin were not coming back. Her brother was gone, and she would be all alone. He pushed that thought to the back of his mind. He would take it out again, when the time was right. He was never an impatient man, and that was the secret of success. A man got what he wanted by waiting for the right time. Long ago, Dobie Nerich had learned to wait.

He stopped his men several hundred yards from the adobe house and looked at it. He said, "You wait here. I'll ride in and see if we can camp here."

They would camp here. No sheepherder would dare to say no to this large a group. Dobie could not get the thought of women out of his mind. That hot, wicked stirring sprang to full life—and he had to do something about it. It never went away of its own accord.

He frowned as he neared the house. It was odd that no one came out to meet him.

He dismounted and knocked on the door. The silence came back strong after the echoes of his knocking faded. But he had the feeling someone was behind the door, a frightened someone. Probably a woman—left alone and waiting in terror for him to go away. He laughed silently and deep in his throat.

"Hello in there," he called. "I only want to ask permission to camp here."

"Si, Senor. It is all right." The voice was faint, muffled by the thickness of the door.

He grinned at the tremulous, feminine voice.

He stood patiently, knowing that she was probably appraising him through a window or some peephole. He knew how harmless he looked, a fat man standing hat in hand.

The door timorously opened a few inches, partially exposing her to his desire. She was young, not over fifteen or sixteen, but developed—provocative in the low-cut blouse. Her dark eyes were soft and big and frightened. And his instinct had been right. She was alone.

13

VINCE ASKED, "How bad, Ron?"

Goddard said through clenched teeth, "It isn't inside, but it burns like hell."

Vince removed the vest and shirt. The shirt was sopping with blood, and Goddard still bled profusely. Vince mopped blood away before he could see the wound. Goddard was right about its severity. The slug had not entered the body cavity, and the relief made Vince weak. The bullet had plowed along a rib, digging a nasty, painful furrow. It was not serious, but it would cause Goddard painful inconvenience.

The men gathered around them, and Vince said, "Surround that house. I don't want whoever's inside getting away."

Austin asked a question, and Vince said, "No, Goddard isn't hurt too bad."

"You think we got Dobie cornered in that house?" Driscoe asked.

"Maybe," Goddard grunted. "And maybe not. We know Dobie's got a bunch with him. Where are their horses? It's open all around the house. And that small shed couldn't hold more than three or four head. Dobie's not going to let himself get caught on foot like this."

"Then who fired on us?" Vince demanded.

"I don't know." Goddard stared at the house with flinty eyes. "But we're sure as hell going to find out."

He looked at Mendoza. "Is this Ceron, this countryman of yours, that unfriendly? Does he shoot at everyone approaching his house?"

Mendoza scowled at the house. "Something is not right, Roque is a peaceful man." He straightened and started forward, waving his hat and shouting in Spanish.

Vince yelled at him, and if Mendoza heard, he did not turn his head, nor pause. Each step made a better target of him, and Vince said with angry worry, "He'll get his head blown off."

Mendoza was well toward the house now, walking slowly, and Vince could not help the quick and ugly suspicion brushing his mind. Whoever was in the house had fired on them. But they were not shooting at Mendoza. Vince could hear Mendoza's voice but could not make out his words. Was he identifying himself with the men in the house; was he leaving Vince and joining them?

Goddard was sitting up, his eyes squinted as he watched. He looked at Vince and shook his head, and Vince thought, The same suspicions are in his mind.

Vince moved to his horse and came back with his

rifle. He lay down and snugged the butt to his shoulder. The sights centered on Mendoza's back. It was a long shot, but he had a steady position. He waited with his finger touching the trigger.

When Mendoza was fifty yards from the house, Vince saw a man leave it and approach him. They held a long and earnest conference, and the sights of the rifle never left Mendoza's back.

Mendoza turned and signaled vigorously. There was no mistaking what Mendoza wanted; he wanted Vince to join him.

A bleak smile was on Goddard's face. "I was thinking like you were. It doesn't take much mistrust to poison a man's mind. Now I'm thinking differently. They've had trouble at that house. Go on. We'll cover you."

Vince moved forward, his rifle ready. He was a clear and open target; exposed as he was, his readiness and the readiness of the men behind him could not stop a slug aimed and fired at him. His skin was tight with painful anticipation of a bullet.

As he neared he saw that the man talking to Mendoza was also Mexican. The man's browned, leathery face was heavy with worry, but the eyes were two fiery coals.

Mendoza said, "Senor Vince, this is Roque Ceron. He thinks we are also enemies. He has had bad trouble here. While Roque and his esposa were away yesterday, many men ride up here. One of them harmed Roque's daughter."

Ceron spoke rapidly, half in Spanish and half in broken English. Vince had trouble following him.

"My wife and son and I drive yesterday to see how the sheep are in the big pasture some twenty miles from here. I expected to return before dark last night. But I break the wheel and cannot get back until this morning. I find my daughter—" His face worked fiercely, and Vince thought he would break into tears. "I kill the pig who does this," Ceron said.

Mendoza said, "Just before Senor Goddard is shot, I think I see a woman duck from a window. Women should not be shooting at us. So I come closer to ask why." His teeth flashed in a mirthless smile. "It is a fortunate thing Roque recognizes me. I do not blame them for shooting at anyone who comes near."

Vince turned and lifted his rifle high, waving his men on in. He saw Goddard limping slowly along behind them.

They made a ring around Ceron, and he again told his story. Vince heard the enraged murmur grow as they understood him.

"Many men come, *señores*," Ceron said. "My daughter she do not know how many."

Goddard asked, "They were Americanos?"

Ceron bobbed his head. "*Si*, my daughter she say yes. We thought you were those men returning. We wanted to kill you."

Vince heard the low, angry swearing from the listening men. "Is your daughter all right?" The question was ill put, and he fumbled, trying to right it. "I mean is she—is—"

Ceron understood. "My wife is attending her, Senor. She is a capable woman."

Goddard said, "I think they are the men we are hunting. Is it possible to talk to your daughter?"

Ceron's face brightened. "If you are after those hombres, I think it best you talk to her. I did not know what to do. My son and I are only two against many."

Goddard jerked his head at Vince, and Vince followed him into the house. The girl could not have been over seventeen. She lay in bed, covered by a blanket, and her mother hovered protectively over her. The son stood near the door, his face sullen, his eyes hate-filled as he looked at Vince and Goddard. He was young, and all Americanos were the same to him.

Ceron said, "These are friends. They hunt the men who do this."

The son still glowered, but some of the fierceness left the mother's face.

Fear and shock still gripped the girl, and it was difficult for her to fashion her words. Goddard spoke gently to her, and the compassion in that granite face was something to see. He had a daughter, not a great deal older than this girl, and Vince thought he was probably thinking of that daughter.

"How many men were here?" Goddard asked.

"I do not know how many remained outside." Her voice was faint, and Goddard bent close to catch it. "Twelve. Maybe more. The fat man kept coming back to the door. Only he broke into the house."

"Was he bearded? Did you hear a name?"

"Much beard," the girl said. "I think I remember

a name. I think he called himself Robie."

Goddard and Vince locked eyes. Dobie Nerich. Bored with the dull hours of waiting, and happening by here, to find this girl alone.

Goddard touched her shoulder. "We will kill the fat man for you."

The girl suddenly sobbed and buried her face in her mother's breast.

"Out," the mother said fiercely to the men in the room. "All of you. Out."

Outside the house Goddard said, "Dobie's running up a hell of a bill."

"It's time to collect it," Vince said. He was abandoning the horse hunt. It was not important against this. For the first time in his life he could think of killing a man and find savage delight in the thought. He looked at the waiting men. "They're ready, too."

Goddard shook his head. "Nothing's changed since we started. We still have to find them. Are you ready to spend weeks in finding him?" His voice roughened. "Don't you think I want Morgan as bad as the rest of you want Dobie?"

Ceron stood to one side, puzzledly watching the argument. Goddard called him over. He asked, "Do you know where we look for this fat hombre?"

Ceron shrugged, the hopelessness big on his face. "If I knew, Senor, do you think I would be here? For many days the tracking of anything has been bad. The wind, she is busy. Always busy."

Goddard looked at Vince, and his expression said, Things are the same.

He told Ceron why they were here. "The fat man is watching us, waiting until we have collected the horses. Then he plans to take them away from us."

A fire was burning in Ceron's eyes. "Si, si," he said excitedly. "Catching the horses will bring them to us. It will be quicker than trying to find them. It is the only way. Last week, I saw the great stallion. In a little valley not too far from here. He will not move. Not as long as the grass is good and he is not frightened. I go with you. When the fat man comes, he is mine."

Goddard glanced at Vince, and Vince nodded. If Ceron thought this way was best, Vince could not set himself against it. And Ceron certainly had the right to go with them. But it went against the grain to calmly go about normal business, when this thing ate at a man's mind.

He asked Ceron, "Shouldn't I leave someone to watch your wife and daughter?"

Ceron shook his head, and his tone was bitter. "A man does not return after such a thing as this. Besides, my son and wife will watch. It was my wife who shot Senor Goddard."

Vince looked back as they rode away. The little adobe house looked lonely and unprotected. He saw Ceron look back, then stare straight ahead, his face set in harsh, bitter lines.

14

THE FOLLOWING afternoon, they spotted the herd from the brow of an overhanging cliff. The wild horses were three or four miles to the south and appeared as mere dots grazing slowly over the valley floor. Vince felt the hard pound of excitement within him. He had never seen so many horses gathered into a single band. At a rough guess he would say there were close to two hundred head. He looked around at the intent faces, the eyes shining with the same excitement he felt.

Ceron said almost reverently, "It is the great horse. Caballo Padre."

Caballo Padre had picked his range well. The flat valley contained abundant grass, and three streams cut through it. The valley, beneath Vince, narrowed into a canyon which ran for several hundred yards, then ended against the steep face of the cliff. It would make a natural corral, and the entrance could be closed by a few men on guard, or by stretching ropes across it. The valley appeared to be almost circular in shape, perhaps six miles in diameter. From here he could see only two exits. They would have to be checked and plugged. If they could drive the herd at top speed around the basin until they reached the canyon mouth, they would have tired horses to handle, with most of the fight taken out of them. It would take breakneck riding and a constant change of fresh mounts, and Vince accordingly mapped his campaign.

It was too late in the afternoon to start the run, and after the evening meal was over, Vince drew a diagram of his plans in the sand. Goddard and Driscoe were to be the supply men, handling the fresh horses. Driscoe grumbled about his part; he would have preferred to be in the chase. Vince said, "Hobe, your part is probably the most important of all. You keep fresh horses at the right spot, and the hunt is a success. You miss, and we're through."

That pacified Driscoe. Goddard was agreeable to his share. His wound would stand no hard riding. Vince designated points in his sand map at where he wanted the fresh mounts.

"We'll run them until they're ready to drop. You two pick up the winded horses, get them water and grain, and keep replacing them."

The terrain would be helpful to his plans. After the exits from the valley floor were plugged, the wild herd would race around the valley, cut off from escape by the steepness of the surrounding cliffs. Vince and his men would run the herd around the basin as though it were a huge race track. At any time, the riders could cut across the complete circle, or cut a partial arc, saving time and energy,

energy that the wild horses were expending in their effort to escape.

Vince doubted there was much sleep in camp that night. He lay on the ground, staring up at the sky. The hunt was going to be a success. He felt it. He wondered where Nerich was, and if he were under Dobie's eye. He hoped he was. He wanted Nerich to come to him. He had one last thought before he dropped off into uneasy sleep. He wished Colin could have seen this bunch.

They made their start before dawn the following day, carefully working their way down and behind the last place they had seen the horses. He put the two Clayton brothers in the exits from the valley floor. If the wild horses attempted to use them, a screaming, waving man—firing rifles, if necessary —would turn them back onto the valley floor.

Men kept dropping out, taking their spots— ready to dash out when the herd swept by, to run at it and keep it moving at top speed with fresh horses. Before it was fully light, Vince and Austin were directly behind the herd. Ahead of them, they heard uneasy snorting and the scrape of hoofs on rocks. Vague, blurred shadows began to take on definite outline and to stand out as individual horses.

Then the light swelled over the eastern rim, and Vince saw the black stallion, El Caballo Padre. The stallion stood a few hundred yards ahead of him, its fore legs moving in uneasy rhythm, its head held high, the little spike ears pointed forward, its nostrils testing the morning breeze. It was uneasy but not frightened for the horse did not as yet see the approaching men. When it saw them, the unease would change to fright. Vince kept that easy forward pace toward him. The stallion snorted, reared, and pawed the air. All around him mares had stopped grazing, and their heads lifted as they waited in anxious wariness for the stallion's decision.

The stallion bugled, then whirled, his fore hoofs slashing the soil. The powerful hind quarters exploded him forward, and he was in full stride. The wind whipped back his mane and tail, and he was as pretty to watch as a mountain stream.

Vince swept off his hat and yelled in sheer exultation. Better than two hundred horses were galloping madly before him and Austin. They spurred after them, slowly turning the herd in the first arc of the great circle. Other riders spurred out and took up the chase as Vince's and Austin's horses grew winded.

The hunted and the hunter equally knew no respite. The relentless pressure must be kept on the wild horses. Never give them a second's rest, a chance to pause and ease laboring lungs, nor the opportunity to thrust slavering muzzles into cool water. That kind of pressure meant equal self-imposed pressure on the hunters. His mounts got refreshing rest and water, but there was none for him. Just the wind alone was part of the physical punishment. It plastered a man's clothes tight to his body and whipped his face and body with soft unremitting blows, unnoticed until the accumulation of them piled high. The wind slapped at a man's face, and the saddle clubbed at his backsides, and muscles began to scream under the punishment.

Vince scrambled through the shallow streams, climbed the gentle rises of the valley floor, then thundered down on the other side. When a horse began to labor, he swung out of the saddle and ran toward a fresh mount. It was grab the horn and swing up, and they were off again. The wild exultation of the first few moments was gone, trampled by the demanding necessities of the drive. The excitement and purpose were still there, but deadened in exact proportion to the pounding taken by flesh. A man took a terrible beating in a chase like this. But he would not really know how tired and trembling his muscles were until the drive was over.

They ran the herd through most of the morning; they ran them until the will to run was gone. The great reaching strides were only a shambling shuffle, and even the stallion could find no more than a slow gallop. They could be herded at will, turned in any direction, and there was no resistance in them. A few, during the chase, had turned back and broken through, and Vince let them go. Now all the men participating in the run were behind and round the herd, moving it toward the mouth of the canyon, intent on threading it through that narrow entrance. Occasionally, one of the wild horses made a feeble dash for freedom, but it was only token resistance, quickly subdued by the fresher horses of the riders.

As they approached the canyon, the riders on the flanks of the herd dropped back, reinforcing the line of men pushing the herd toward the opening. The wild horses pressed close together in mutual fear and exhaustion. The stallion still trotted out ahead of the others, but his head hung low, and his coat was lathery with sweat. These were tired, dragging horses, and there should be no trouble in corralling them.

He was so close to success that Vince wanted to yell with it. He held it until the last of the wild ones stumbled into the canyon. Two men darted out from the covering brush and closed the entrance with tightly stretched ropes. He could yell now. It was done.

He found the effort it took to yell was not in him. He grinned vacantly as he climbed down from the saddle. He was stiff with fatigue, and every muscle set up a clamoring protest. They had done it. In one huge drive they had corralled more than enough horses to fill the contract. He looked at the men. He saw their stiff, wooden-like motions that spoke of complete weariness. Their faces were masklike, hardened in the harsh mold of fatigue. But a spark still burned in their eyes, a spark lit by the knowledge of success.

Goddard came over and looked at the herd, packed into the small canyon. The spark was in his eyes, too. No man could look on that many horses without feeling a swelling in his heart and a corresponding tightening in his throat.

He said, "We've got them this far. Now we'll learn if we can hold them."

The grim note in his voice brought Vince sharply

back to reality. Not once during the chase had he thought of Dobie Nerich and the covetous eyes that might be watching them. He asked, "Have you seen anything?"

Goddard shook his head. "Nothing. But I feel like there's something crawling up my back."

15

VINCE SCOWLED at the distant, brooding hills. He
knew what Goddard meant. The same feeling was
with him. Dobie Nerich was somewhere in those
hills. Goddamn him, Vince thought. It was a big
thought; it was an effort to keep from screaming it.

He said, "They'll probably wait until we do the
rest of the hard work. They'll let us break the horses
and get them ready to bring in."

"Don't depend on it," Goddard warned. "They
can make their try at any time."

Vince looked at him with hooded eyes. "I'm not."
From now on, every moment would be doubly
guarded. He said, "Ron, while we start the breaking, take Ceron and Mendoza with you. Pick a point
high enough so that you can see every approach."

Goddard nodded and moved lamely toward his
horse. He drew his rifle from its scabbard and called
Mendoza and Ceron to him. Vince saw their bob-
bing heads as Goddard talked; then the three
started their climb. He did not think an attack
would come during the day, but he would allow no

111

careless assumption to lull him into a false security. Ceron would watch well, and Goddard equally so. They had reasons driving them.

He mounted, shook out his rope, and headed toward the corral. Driscoe lowered the ropes, and Vince rode inside. He cut quietly through the wild herd, and the horses were too tired to do more than draw a few feet away from him. He neared the black stallion and built his loop. It slipped through the air with a soft, whispering sigh and dropped over the sweat-stained neck.

One last explosive bit of strength was left in the stallion. Its eyes rolled, showing the muddy whites, and its ears whipped forward and back. It reared, walking on its hind hoofs, slashing out with the front ones. Its shrill, angry trumpeting filled the corral, and for an instant the herd panicked, running wildly in all directions, then bunching together again at the end of the canyon. Vince's horse threw its weight against the stallion, pulling it back to the ground. It kept the rope taut, draining the last fading resistance from the stallion. It stood trembling and slowly its head drooped.

Vince dismounted and went hand over hand up the rope, keeping up a soothing, gentle monotone. He reached out and touched the horse. Its muscles quivered under his fingers, and that was all.

Two men came up with shorter ropes, swapped ropes with Vince, and led the stallion away to hobble it. Other riders were working through the herd cutting out and roping the best of the animals. The scrubs were hazed toward the rope barrier and released. They found energy enough for one last frenzied dash away from this terrifying, confining place.

When an animal was roped and subdued, a man hobbled and led it away, to put it with the growing bunch that Vince considered cavalry caliber. It was the beginning of the animal's education, and the first topping would follow tomorrow.

They quit work when it was too dark to safely see. The last few hours' work was only a sample of what would follow. Each horse had to be roped again, tamed a little, saddled and bridled for the first time in its life, then broken. To the fatigue of aching muscles would be added bruises, and if a man's luck was bad, very probably broken bones. When it was over, each horse would have been ridden at least once—twice, if time permitted. They would be by no means gentle horses, but any rider with a little skill and nerve could ride them. The cavalry liked their horses full of fire, and Vince grinned wearily as he thought they are going to get a big handful of just that.

He picked four men as guards on the first shift to midnight. He hated the necessity of it, for these were tired men. He laid out a beat for each one and told them to slowly patrol it. It was necessary for them to keep moving, for men as weary as they were could go to sleep standing on their feet.

He came back to the dying fire and rolled a last cigarette before turning in. Goddard squatted before the fire, poking the failing embers together. He glanced at Vince and said, "Ceron's gone."

He saw the flash of alarm in Vince's eyes and said, "He'll be all right. He wasn't content to just sit and wait. There's too much wild blood in him. Maybe it's a good thing to have him out there prowling around. Maybe he will be able to spot which direction it will come from and be able to give us a little warning." He was silent for a long moment. "I hope so. There won't be any room for mistakes."

Vince gloomily nodded. He was afraid Goddard was right.

He rolled up in his blankets, and worry kept sleep away. He worried about Dobie Nerich and where he was. Would an attack come soon, or would it wait until the hard, sweaty work of breaking the horses was over? What direction would it come from and what time? He rolled over, cursing softly. Unanswerable questions like those could drive a man crazy.

He knew nothing else until Goddard was shaking him awake. He sat up and shivered as the chill night air bit into him. "Time to walk a little," Goddard said.

Vince yawned as he pulled on his boots. He got sleepily to his feet and went out and relieved Dan Abel.

Abel said, "I thought you were never coming. I'm dead."

Vince nodded. He knew how Abel felt. And the sad part of it was that Abel would feel no better in the morning. Four hours sleep was not enough for tired muscles that screamed out for more.

Mendoza had one of the beats, and each time Vince met him, they exchanged a few words. He told him what Goddard said about Ceron and saw the gleam of Mendoza's teeth in the night.

"Si," Mendoza said. "Roque told me. He did not come to you because he was afraid you would not let him go. Do not worry about him. He is a good man to have out there. He knows this country as well as his hand. He can see more and better than any of us walking here."

Vince nodded and turned. He heard the scrape of hoofs below him as a tired horse moved, heard a dry cough coming from a sleeping man. His hands gripped the rifle, wanting the intensity of the pressure to flag his dull senses into more alertness. Methodically and slowly, he moved through the night, so many steps one way, so many another.

He had known short nights in his life, but this was not one of them. When dawn finally broke, he thought he had just finished the longest night he would ever spend. And there were more of the same kind ahead of him.

The roping, tying, taming and breaking went on for five days. A man was lucky to go through a day without being dumped at least a time or two. Everyone knew minor sprains and bruises, and the man who did not limp around camp was a novelty. Caballo Padre threw Vince three straight times before he was able to stick. His guts hurt after he finally rode him, and his mouth was filled with blood. He knew one thing for certain— Caballo Padre was the most horse he ever rode, even topping the sorrel. He might sell the Army the sorrel but not Caballo Padre.

Ceron came in that night. His masklike face hid the weariness of his body, though his heavy movements spoke eloquently of it.

Vince waited until Ceron finished eating before he tried to talk to him. The man ate as though he were starved. He gave Vince a half apologetic smile and said, "I did not take enough food with me. I ate the last of it last night. I did not dare try to shoot at anything."

Vince asked, "More?" and held out the skillet to him.

Ceron shook his head. He saw the big question in Vince's eyes and answered it. "I see nothing. I spend the time looking and waiting, knowing how far a man can see movement. They must know of this, too, for I see nothing. I move during the night to a new place of looking. And again I see nothing."

Vince thought of the lonely hours this man had spent—the hot, silent hours of day, the chilling, silent hours of night. Ceron's was the hardest way, for at the camp they had work to fill their hours. There was no complaint in Ceron. His hating was too big for discomfort to touch him.

"You think they might have given up?" Vince asked.

Ceron's eyes blazed. "They have not given up. They are waiting out there. Each day the tightness here," he put his hand to his throat, then to his heart, "and here, grows more."

Vince soberly nodded. Ceron lived close to this

land, and a man would be foolish to scoff at his instincts.

"How much work do you have left?" Ceron asked.

"A couple of days at the most."

"The teeth of time are sharpening," Ceron said. "They will let you do all the work for them. Then they will come." His tone said his belief was unshakable in that.

He straightened and said, "I will go back. The waiting will not be long now."

Vince said gruffly, "Watch yourself, Roque."

Ceron gave him a brief nod and a faint smile. "You do the same, Amigo."

The night swallowed his figure. Vince sat there, listening. He thought he heard the scrape of a horse's hoof. A shiver ran scaly-footed over his skin. There was depth to Ceron's hating. An ordinary man could not hold hating in him that long without something weakening it. Nothing would weaken Ceron's.

16

CERON'S THOUGHTS were busy as he rode. He would ride far tonight and in a new direction. And tomorrow might bring a distant stirring that his eyes could catch. These were clever men somewhere out there, skillful in the art of keeping themselves hidden. "But we will find them, Elodia," he said aloud. "We will find them, and then the fat hombre will harm no more women."

It would be easy to hate all Americanos for what the fat one had done. But that would be wrong. That kind of hating would include the Senores Vince and Goddard, and all the others who were trying to help him. He must remember to tell his son this. Miguel was young, and the young's hating was blind and all-inclusive. It did not take the time to sort and pick; to reason. If one gringo was bad, then all gringos were bad. Yes, he must remember to talk to Miguel.

He slept the last hours of the night in a depression hollowed out in the sand. He did not curse the chillness that searched out his bones; he did not curse the necessity that forbade him a fire. He stolidly accepted those things.

He was awake with the first light of dawn, his eyes searching the desert from his high location, seeking the tiniest bit of movement, or an alien dot that did not belong there. He could feel time's sharp teeth gnawing on him. Had he guessed wrong again, coming in this direction? But the tightness he spoke of to Senor Vince—it was stronger. It was almost like a band clamping around his chest and throat.

He stayed there until the first purple shadows of evening began to creep over the land, cutting observation to a scant hundred yards. It would be safe to move now, for hostile eyes could observe him no farther than he could observe them.

He rode slowly, keeping his eyes on the desert floor, hoping to see a trace of the passage of man. In a few more minutes he would be unable to see anything.

He saw a scattering of round, dark objects a little distance to his right, and pulled his horse to a stop. He knew what they were before he reached them, and the increased beat of his heart said, Here is the first sign.

He squatted beside the horse droppings and turned them over with a stick. The end of the stick broke through the day's drying crust. He would say they had been dropped some time this morning. Horse droppings by themselves were not significant, for this was horse country. He mashed one with the stick, and his eyes gleamed. In the drop-

ping were several kernels of oats, undigested and
passed by the animal. Wild horses did not eat oats.

He moved a dozen yards and found several
blurred tracks made by shod hoofs. He went forty
yards before there was another clear print. He lined
them up, and the direction was a generally north-
easterly one. If they kept on that course, these
tracks would pass a little to the right of the valley in
which Vince and the others worked.

"They are moving," he said softly. "They have
decided the time is near."

He walked along the line of tracks, bending close
to the ground because of the poor light. He found
another set, then a second and third before the light
faded. The direction remained the same.

He was content as he halted. He would sleep well
tonight, and in the morning find the camp of the fat
man—the camp for which he had looked so long.

He was moving before the sun's rim appeared in
the east. He could easily follow the tracks without
dismounting. The wind had been still during the
night, and the soft sand retained well its im-
pressions. Their camp should not be too far up
ahead. There was no urgency driving them. They
would stop early and sleep late.

He left his horse and walked the last mile. He
looked at the camp from a high prominence of
ground. Even from this distance he could pick out
the fat man's bulk; his hands, holding the rifle,
trembled. It was too long a shot to risk, and there
were other people to consider. Senor Goddard had
an interest in this camp, and Senor Vince. Their bill
should be collected as well as his own.

He turned back, crawling until he was sure the rise in the ground protected him. He straightened and walked back to his horse. He mounted and rode, making a half-circle swing of the fat man's camp. He came down on it from the direction he would have ridden had he passed the horse hunters' camp.

A half mile from the camp he stopped and dismounted. He stripped the saddle from the horse, rubbed it thoroughly with the saddle blanket and judged his work. If a man closely examined the animal, he might find the marks of the saddle. He did not think anyone would be that interested. He put his hat on top of the rifle and saddle, scooped out a shallow depression behind a twisted mesquite tree and covered them.

He drew a bandana handkerchief from his pocket and knotted it just about his forehead. He wore a denim jacket and much used jeans, and moccasins on his feet. A gringo's eye would take him for Indian.

He mounted bareback and kicked the horse forward. He rode openly, and he was almost in the middle of the camp before they knew he was near.

He heard startled cries, and two men leaped forward, grabbing his horse by the bridle. Another reached up and jerked him from the animal's back. He would have fallen had not those rough hands held him erect. One of them seized his wrist and twisted his arm, hammer-locking his hand between his shoulder blades. He did not cry out, but the hurt was in his eyes. He was propelled forward toward the fat man.

"Look what rode in here, Dobie," the man, holding him, said.

Nerich swore and yelled, "How'd he get by Thompson?"

The man laughed and said, "I guess Sull went back to sleep. Hell, Dobie," he protested. "There ain't no harm in him. He's just a Goddamned wandering Indian."

"Let go of him," Dobie ordered.

Ceron's arm fell to his side. For a moment, the relief hurt as much as the actual twisting. He expressed his appreciation in a rapid burst of Mexican, mixed with Indian words. He doubted that the fat man would understand. He was an arm's length from him, and his fingers ached with the desire to rip out his throat.

He was right about the fat one not understanding. Dobie said impatiently, "Can't you talk any English?"

He bobbed his head several times. "A little."

"Where'd you come from?"

Ceron turned and pointed in the direction of the horse hunters' camp.

"See anyone last night or this morning?"

"I see white men," Ceron said brokenly. He held out the fingers of his two hands. "That many. They have many horses."

"Ah," Nerich said with satisfaction. "He passed them all right. Were they getting ready to move?"

Ceron shook his head in negation. "They are much drunk for days, and I think more days to come."

His voice took on a whining note. "I ask for just a little whisky. One drink." He half turned and pointed a forefinger at his rear. "They kick me here."

Somebody broke into raucous laughter, and the fat one yelled, "Quiet!" He stared at Ceron and said, "Indian, I'll give you a bottle, if you can show me the best way to ride into their camp without them knowing we're near."

Ceron eagerly nodded and squatted on his heels. With his finger he drew a map in the sand. The fat man looked over his shoulder, his breathing fanning his cheek. Dios Mio—to be this close to him and to do nothing about it!

He drew a picture of the valley with its sealed canyon end. "The horses are there."

A short, chunky, wide-shouldered man said, "Dobie, I told you that!"

Nerich waved him still with an impatient hand. "This Indian's been there all right, Hoyt. Do we use the canyon?" he asked.

Ceron vigorously shook his head. "This arroyo leads down from the mountain into the valley." He drew another line in the sand, bisecting the outline of the valley. "It will hide many men until they are close to the camp."

Nerich straightened, his eyes gleaming. "If their whisky holds out, they'll be drunk again tonight. I guess it's time to move."

He straightened and said, "Hoyt. Give him a bottle."

"It's a waste of whisky," Morgan grumbled. But

he rummaged in a saddle bag, produced a bottle and tossed it to Ceron.

Ceron faced the fat man, his face beaming. He said his "Gracias" over and over. He did not see Morgan move up behind him.

A hard kick sent him sprawling. He looked around, and Morgan was grinning. Laughter was on all their faces. "Indian," Morgan said, "we did not want you thinking we weren't as hospitable as they were."

Even the fat man was laughing. "I'd run, Indian," he advised. "Before they show you more hospitality."

Ceron picked up his bottle and ran for his horse. They were still laughing as he mounted and kicked his horse into a full run. This Indian knew better than to hang around a white man's camp.

17

ANOTHER day at the most would see the job of breaking completed. They had kept a hundred and fifteen horses from the wild herd. Vince had culled them carefully, and he did not think Simas would reject any of them. But Simas had only ordered a hundred horses. Vince knew what to do with the surplus. He called the Clayton brothers, Hall and Driscoe over to the corral. Abel, Austin and Mendoza were on guard. They could make their choice later.

He said, "Pick out a head apiece. I figure you got a right to do your picking before the Army does."

They incredulously stared at him, for a moment not comprehending what he was doing. Stu Hall asked in a not quite steady voice, "You mean you're giving us a horse apiece?"

Vince frowned at him. "That's what I meant. Pick from everything but the stallion. Of course, if you don't want—"

Their whoops of joy washed over the remainder of his words. He did not expect direct thanks. It

would come in little, offhand ways, in some added
special they could find to do for him. As he turned
away they were already wrangling over the respec-
tive merits of this animal against that one. A few
moments ago, they had looked at these animals
with a sour eye, for they meant only work and
bruises. Now there was a new light in those eyes.
Four of these horses were theirs. Each would spend
hours in making a choice, then go back and do it
over.

He moved to where Goddard was sitting and
said, "Ron, that goes for you, too."

Goddard asked, "You figger you have to buy me,
too?"

He grinned at the indignation swelling in Vince's
face. "Vince," he said, "I'd died sure as hell, if you
hadn't made me the same offer."

He chuckled as Driscoe's voice carried to them.
"You're crazy as hell," Driscoe yelled. "You mean
that knot-headed thing compares with that bay."

"I'm no more crazy than you're blind," Stu Hall
said hotly.

They would argue the rest of the day, but it
would be a different kind of argument than what
had been going on. This would be the argument of
companionship.

Goddard said, "You did a smart thing, Vince.
Their tempers were getting ragged. Look how they
snapped at each other this morning. Some of them
wouldn't speak at all."

Vince nodded. That had not been in his mind
when he submitted to a generous impulse, but it

126

would work for him. This would wipe out all the friction the short hours of sleep and the long hours of toil had created.

He said, "We're going to have a job getting them back. I figure on tying the lead mares to some of the tame stock. I'll put Caballo Padre between two of us. I guess we'll make out."

Goddard's eyes were lifted to the rim of the hills. How often all of them did that. "We'll make it," he said.

Vince groaned as he reached for his saddle. "I'm so damned sore I can tell you if a fly crawls across the seat of my pants. And there's about a dozen head in there that needs some more work."

Goddard grinned. "I guess I was pretty smart in getting myself shot."

Vince said sourly, "Smarter than the rest of us."

As he lay down that night, he thought, It's over. Except for the trip back to town. He would be within his limit of thirty days. And Dobie Nerich had not materialized. Was all his worry over him for nothing? He could not believe that. Would Nerich hit them while they were moving? Was he setting up an ambush somewhere up ahead? He fell asleep still asking himself questions he could not answer.

He slapped at the hand shaking him awake. He was to go on guard at midnight, and he knew it could not be that time yet.

Goddard said in his ear, "Ceron just came in. Vince, you hear me?"

The sleep fog was wiped from Vince's mind. He

sat up and asked, "What's he say?"

"He'll tell you," Goddard grunted.

Ceron was at the fire, drinking a cup of coffee. He set the cup down and said, "Last night, I found a horse dropping."

Vince said, "The country's full of horses." Partial anger was in his voice. Did Ceron think that was news?

Ceron's grin had a wolf quality to it. "Amigo," he softly asked, "do the wild horses eat grain? There was grain in that dropping." He heard the sound of Vince's increased breathing. "Ah, you see it. Mexicans and Indians do not feed grain to their horses. Our horses were here."

He paused, enjoying their attention.

"Go on," Vince snapped.

"I followed the trail of those horses. This morning, I rode into their camp."

"You saw them, and they let you go?" At Ceron's nod, Vince said, "Good God! The chance you took."

Ceron's teeth bared in a mirthless grin. "They did not know me. I rode in bareback. They took me for an Indian begging for whisky."

Vince could see how easy that would be. "It was Dobie Nerich's camp?"

"Si. The fat man with the big beard."

"How many men, Roque?"

"Counting the fat one, sixteen. The fat man asked many questions. I am angry with the horse hunters. They did not give me whisky, and they booted me from their camp. I tell him everything he wants to know." He picked up a short stick and drew a heavy line in the sand. His tone was soft but deadly. "This is the deep arroyo that leads down to the valley floor. I tell the fat man the horse hunters are much drunk with their success. That they have plenty more whisky and the drinking will go on. The arroyo will hide him until he is in the middle of a drunken camp." His teeth bared again. "I picked up another small bill to collect with the greater one. They gave me my whisky; then the one called Hoyt booted me."

"Morgan," Goddard said.

Vince nodded. That would appeal to Morgan's twisted humor. "When, Roque?" he asked.

"I think tonight, or perhaps early in the morning, when the light is good."

Vince turned his head and stared in the direction of the arroyo. If he wanted to hit an unsuspecting camp in this valley, it was the approach he would take. Nerich would have numerical superiority, but the surprise would be on a different side than he expected.

He said, "Thanks, Roque."

Ceron shrugged. "I have the bigger reason than you."

Goddard's voice sounded hungry. "They're coming to us, Vince." This was the moment Goddard had been living for.

Vince moved out and alerted the guard, telling them what was ahead. By the time he returned, Goddard and Ceron had awakened the others. They huddled in the chilly night. There would be no fire, no warming cup of coffee. The tension strung them tight. They talked in soft whispers, when they spoke. The tension would worsen before it slackened.

Goddard went to the wagon and came back with his arms filled with molasses jugs. Some of them were empty. From the distance, they looked like the kind of jugs used for whisky.

"If they want to find a drunken camp, we'll give them one," he said. "We don't want to disappoint Dobie in anything. We need some drunks to lay around. Help me make some dummies."

They gathered dry grass and stuffed it into spare trousers and shirts, then laid hats on the upper end of the grotesque figures. They sprawled the dummies over the area, as though they were sleeping off a big spree. Some lay partially in bedrolls. Others were tumbled on the ground as though they had not been quite able to make it to their bedrolls.

The jugs were placed conspicuously near the sleeping figures. Even a fairly close inspection gave the illusion of a tremendous celebration after a successful hunt. When Dobie Nerich looked down on this camp, the open invitation of big gains at no cost should draw him unsuspectingly all the way.

They walked to the arroyo that Nerich would use —according to Ceron. This was a gamble, staking everything on a calculated risk. By watching this approach, the others would be left open. But Vince was sure Nerich would avail himself of the wandering Indian's information. He felt a heavy, cold numbness. They had set another trap, but this time it was for man, and the thought stuck burr-like in his mind.

Goddard guessed his thoughts and said, "It never sets well. But some men need killing worse than any animal. That bunch hope to murder ten sleeping men."

Vince growled, "Do you think I'm regretting anything?"

They picked their positions on higher ground, about halfway up the wash. They scrambled up the sides, finding cover behind rock and brush. Goddard lifted his voice to carry to the men on the other side of the arroyo, "Don't shoot until I do. I look for them right after dawn."

Vince crouched between two boulders. Dawn was a long way off, but already his eyes were beginning to ache with the strain of trying to penetrate the darkness. The ache in his fingers spread through his hands, until he realized how hard he was gripping his rifle. He forced himself to relax. This waiting to kill a man in this manner was the heaviest pressure he had ever known. He wished he could light a cigarette.

18

THE BLACKNESS thinned to an early, sullen gray; a
bush, twenty feet away, that he could not see before
came into vague view. Vince saw Goddard's blurred
form, lying behind a rock to his right, and as the
light strengthened he picked out other forms on the
other side of the arroyo. The sullen gray gave way
to a lesser shade; then the rising sun poured tints of
pink and gold into the morning. Across the arroyo,
a man stirred restlessly, dislodging a small pebble.
It rolled down the slope to the arroyo floor, and its
clatter seemed as loud as that a big boulder would
make. Vince hissed sharply, and the deadly quiet
was unbroken again.

He thought he heard the soft sighing of the wind
and looked around. But there was no wind; not a
blade nor leaf was stirring. He looked at Goddard,
and Goddard was making the soft, sighing sound
and jerking his head toward the high promontory
that overlooked the entire valley. Vince stared in the
direction Goddard wanted him to, and his eyes
could pick out nothing alien. Then movement pin-

pointed it for him. He saw a tiny blob move back
from the skyline. It had been the slightest of movements, gone so quickly a man could not be certain
he saw it. That tiny moving dot against the light
could have been a man's head, a head cautiously
raised over the crest and surveying the camp below.
He looked back at Goddard and knew he was not
mistaken in seeing the moving dot. The savage
triumph in Goddard's face said he had seen it, too.
Goddard's words carried to him as the faintest of
whispers. "They'll be coming now."

The waiting was on them again, the waiting that
stretched a man's nerves until he wanted to howl
under the strain of it. But not a man broke under
the harsh, self-imposed discipline. Vince saw not a
movement from his force, and not a word carried to
him. Half of them were on one side of the arroyo,
half on the other, scattered out for a distance of fifty
yards. Dobie Nerich and his outfit would ride into a
deadly crossfire, poured into them from above. If
they came. Vince could not sidestep the disturbing
question. But they might not come. Something
might happen to veer them away. Suppose they
caught something unreal about the drunken camp?
That would make Nerich change his mind. Vince
had no doubt the camp had been under glasses
since it was light enough to see. The magnifying
power of the glasses could have picked up a false
detail. Was Nerich passing up this morning in favor
of another time, another spot? If he did not come
this morning, the route to town would be a strained
and jumpy way, for this empty country would lend

itself to countless numbers of ambushes. If surprise
was taken away from Vince, those extra men of
Nerich's would count heavily.

Goddard's face was gray and haggard under the
waiting, and Vince wondered if the same kind of
thoughts were running through Goddard's mind.
He stiffened as he heard a sharp, clear click, the
click such as a hoof makes in striking a stone.

The sound of his breathing seemed painfully loud
as he waited. Then he heard another click, then a
series of them. The first horseman came into view
around a bend in the arroyo. He was a big, heavy
man with a beard that covered most of his face. Despite his bulk he rode with easy, sure grace, and he
held a ready rifle across the pommel of the
saddle.

Vince's eyes burned as he stared at him. All of
Goddard's suspicions of the man were justified.
Dobie Nerich was here, and the ready rifle was
proof of his intentions.

Other horsemen followed Dobie down the arroyo
in a tight, closed-up line. Vince counted them.
Ceron had been accurate. There were sixteen of
them. All of them rode with their rifles at the ready.

They came down the arroyo at an easy walk, the
hoofs of their mounts clicking against the stones.
They were close enough now for Vince to hear the
creak of saddle leather and the snorting of horses.
He saw the grins of satisfaction on the faces of
Nerich's men and knew what was going through
their minds. Better than ten thousand dollars of
horseflesh waited for them—and drunken men
would put up little or no defense.

Morgan kicked his horse forward and rode with
Nerich. Vince saw him say something to Nerich,
then throw back his head and laugh without sound.
There was the man who had murdered Colin,
murdered him because Colin had hurt his pride. He
could laugh now, even with the intended butchery
filling his head.

Vince glanced at Goddard, expecting to see the
rifle butt snugged against his shoulder. But no personal feeling could stampede Goddard into too
hasty action. He was waiting, waiting until Nerich
and the others were squarely in the middle of the
trap.

They came on down the wash, and the mouth of
the arroyo was before them, opening onto the floor
of the valley. Another hundred yards and the
campsite would be in uncluttered view, perhaps
close enough for them to detect the falseness of the
scene.

Goddard's rifle sights were aligned, but instead
of shooting he yelled, "That's far enough, Dobie.
Drop those guns."

The riders in the arroyo sharply reined in their
horses, forcing them to rear and wheel. Vince saw
the shock of utter astonishment slack the faces
below him. He heard the quick and frightened cursing and knew the surprise was complete. He suspected why Goddard yelled, and was relieved that
he did. Goddard was a lawman, and back-shooting
and ambushing did not sit with him. Now whatever
happened those men brought on themselves.

Morgan was the first to recover. He lifted his rifle
and fired, and the bullet gouged at the boulder left

of Goddard's head, then slashed off into space screaming angrily.

Goddard's answering shot came a flick of time later. Morgan's horse went down, and another rider cut in front of Morgan. Before his view of him was blotted out, Vince saw Morgan with his arms upraised, one hand still holding the rifle. Morgan' motions looked controlled, and Vince doubted he was hit. Downhill shooting made for difficult accuracy. Goddard's bullet was probably too low striking the horse instead of Morgan.

Rifles spat from both sides of the arroyo, and the heavy reports seemed to roll along the arroyo floor until they piled up against the walls with the booming sound of heavy surf. Horses reared and wheeled into each other, their shrill, frightened screaming adding to the noise pounding at the ears. The scene on the arroyo floor was a confused, shifting melee of struggling horses and men. Vince caught Dobie in his sights, pulled the trigger, and the horse was jerked from under the man. He cursed as he levered in another shell. He had made Goddard's mistake shooting too low. He had killed Nerich's horse instead of the man. He shifted his sights, trying to pick up Nerich again, and Nerich was protected by a constantly shifting screen of horses and men.

The wash rocked with the reports of the rifles. A ragged return fire was started by the trapped men below, but most of the shots were wild and unaimed, the fearful instinctive action of men who had no other way to defend themselves. Yelling and swearing swelled up from the arroyo floor, shrill

with a note of fear. A rider threw up his arms and
suddenly came all loose in the saddle. The horse
seemed to run out from under the man, and the
body, for a flick of time, hung in the air. Then it fell
and bounced along the rocky ground, its grotesque
flopping saying the life was poured out of it.

Vince's sights settled on a ducking, spurring
rider. The rifle butt kicked back against his shoulder. It had a much harder kick at the other end. It
kicked that rider out of his saddle, and he fell in a
broken sprawl.

Slugs hummed beelike overhead. He thought he
heard Goddard grunt and turned his head. If Goddard had been hit, it was not bad, for he was tra-
versing the muzzle of his rifle, seeking new targets. A
slug hit into the ground a foot from Vince's head,
rocking and lifting sand and grit, sending it out in
a fanlike spray. Some of it reached Vince's face, and
stung like wind-driven hail. It had force enough
to put water in his eyes, and he wiped at them.

His eyes cleared, and he heard an agonized yelp
from the other bank of the wash. He saw a man lift
and stand against the incline of the slope, his arms
extended as though he were trying to grab support
out of the air. For an instant he stood in a grotesque
parody of prayer; then the arms dropped, and the
man broke at the middle. He fell slowly; then the
slope seized him, building up momentum. He
rolled faster and faster, tumbling all the way to the
bottom. From this distance Vince could not be sure
which one of his men had been killed. It looked like
the blue shirt one of the Clayton boys was wearing,

and something tightened in Vince's throat.

A half dozen riderless horses galloped madly
about below, their unguided courses sending them
blundering and crashing into each other. Another
rider toppled out of the saddle and sprawled heavily
on the rocky ground. The body jumped twice under
the impact of the vengeful fire poured into it from
the slopes above.

Vince shot again and knocked a man out of the
saddle. The man went down in a tumbling heap but
jumped to his feet and ran limpingly to the protec
tion of a great boulder. Vince's slugs kicked up grav
el around the man's feet, but he did not stop him.
He heard the sharp crack of several rifles, and the
man flung out from behind the boulder. He had
been covered from Vince's fire but exposed to the
fire from the other slope. Vince did not fire again.
There was a queer brokenness to that shambling
stride that told him the man was going down for
good. He was already seeking another target as the
man fell.

A half dozen sprawled figures were scattered
about on the arroyo floor. Dobie Nerich's men were
being cut to pieces. Vince saw two riders spurring
madly back up the wash. Rifle slugs searched for
them, but the last he saw of them, they were still in
the saddle, neither of them apparently hit. It made
two less, for those men had no other intention but
to get as far from here as quickly as possible.

Nerich was on foot somewhere down there, and
Vince had not seen Morgan since the first moment.
He saw the evil wink of a rifle flash and heard an

other of his men cry out in pain. That shot came from the other side of the arroyo, from a higher spot even than his men occupied. He scowlingly searched the higher slopes of the wash, hoping that the unseen marksman would fire again so he could pinpoint his location. The sweep of his eyes picked up nothing. He could have been mistaken about that wink of flame.

Two riderless horses tried to climb the steep embankment pawing frantically at the slippery incline, scrambling up a few feet, then sliding back again. One of them turned and went up the canyon, galloping wildly, the stirrups drumming against its barrel with each stride. The other tried to go downhill, and its reins snagged in the brush. It reared and lunged against the restraint, but the reins held, and the horse stood in trembling fear.

Vince thought he saw movement from a jumble of rocks near the horse and shifted for a better view. A bullet whanged into his protective rock, splintering chips and driving one of them into his cheek. The sting and shock of it watered his eyes, and he shook his head, trying to clear his vision. When he saw clearly again, a man was running with a twisting, darting motion toward the imprisoned horse. He knew that massive, bulky figure. Dobie Nerich was making a break for it, running toward the horse caught in the brush. Vince fired twice. He saw the sand pock in front of Nerich, but the man's stride did not falter.

One of Nerich's men, seeing Nerich making a break for a horse, sprang to his feet and rushed in the opposite direction. If he hoped Nerich would divert fire from him, he was wrong. The diversion helped Nerich, swinging the rifles on the heights above him to the second running man. A half dozen bullets punctured him, dropping him in his tracks. But Nerich had succeeded in freeing the reins, and he was in the saddle, spurring downhill. Once he reached the mouth of the arroyo, the valley opened wide before him and he could find his freedom through it.

Rage was a tight band around Vince's throat at the thought of Nerich getting away. He jumped to his feet, forgetting there could be a hidden rifleman across the way, waiting for just such a move. He ran downhill in long, springing bounds. Nerich had reached the brush at the end of the arroyo, and while rifles still spat at him, the screen of brush made for poor shooting.

Other of Vince's men had the same thought—to stop Dobie Nerich. He could see them springing into view all over the slopes and racing downhill. A bullet slammed into Vince's foot, and for a moment he thought the entire foot had been shot away. He went down hard, the sand particles scraping his face. The shock and numbing impact were still in the foot, deadening the pain that would flood it later. He looked and saw that the slug had cleanly taken off the heel of his right boot, throwing him to the ground. That had been an aimed shot, coming from the man on higher ground. An inch higher, and Vince would not be thinking of running. He would be on the ground, writhing in agony.

He yelled, "Look out. He's over there."

It was doubtful anyone heard him, or realized what was happening until Stu Hall went down. Hall's stride broke; he hit the ground and slithered a half dozen feet. That focused attention on the marksman, for men stopped and fired at the cover protecting him. But in the meanwhile, Nerich was getting farther away.

Vince pushed to his feet and ran on with a limping, bucketing stride. His breathing was a gush of liquid fire, and he sobbed as he ran. He would never catch up with Nerich on foot—but he doggedly kept on.

A riderless horse burst out of the tangle of brush ahead of him. It had raced down the arroyo; then, unreasoning in its panic, had whirled and galloped back. Vince made a sprawling leap at the dangling reins, caught them, and was almost jerked off his feet. He dropped his rifle and could not recover it. He managed to haul the horse to a stop and walked up the reins. He got a hand on the horn and as the horse twisted away from him, sprang into the saddle.

He turned the animal and spurred down the arroyo. Back of him, rifles were still barking, but the reports were sporadic instead of continuous. The yells and firing grew fainter as he put distance behind him.

Luck had picked him a good horse. He knew it had speed before the first hundred yards were covered. He burst out onto the valley floor and he saw the fleeing man not too far ahead of him. He thought he heard the drum of hoofs behind him and slewed in the saddle for a quick look. Roque Ceron was behind him, his black hair flying in the air. Ceron, too, had found a horse and was intent that Nerich should not escape. But his horse was slower. In that quick glimpse, Vince thought he saw it lose a little ground.

He settled down to hard riding, spurring and quirting the horse, and in the next ten minutes he materially cut down the gap. He regretted the loss of his rifle. It left him at a disadvantage with only a hand-gun against Nerich's rifle. Nerich was worrying. Every so often, he turned his head watching that narrowing gap.

It took a fast horse a considerable time to cut down even a small lead. Vince wasted no shots in trying to pick off Nerich. At the distance and from the back of a running horse, a hit would be sheer luck. Twice he thought Nerich was going to fire at him, from the way the man swiveled around in his saddle and raised the rifle. But each time he turned back and urged the horse on. He seemed to be veering to the left—and there was no escape that way for the cliff rose sheer ahead of him. Vince was less than three hundred yards behind him, when he saw Nerich's intentions. Nerich was steering toward a slight elevation, covered with boulders and rocks. Even as Vince realized what was in the man's mind, Nerich jerked the horse to a skidding halt and leaped out of the saddle before the horse was fully stopped. He fought for his balance during a half dozen stumbling strides, then was running strongly or the breastwork of rocks. He reached them, and Vince saw him throw himself behind them.

The advantage was all Nerich's, and Vince was tempted to jump from the saddle and seek cover, too. Thinking frantically, he decided it would do him no good. It would mean a long stalk, considering he could even get close enough to Nerich to effectively use his pistol. His best chance was to keep coming in, gambling on the fact that a man on a running horse made a difficult target.

He heard the crack of the rifle and saw the spurt of muzzle flame. The bullet hit in front of his horse, throwing up a small geyser of sand and grit. Vince leaned close to the horse's neck, making himself as small as possible. The sheer foolhardiness of his charge must have unnerved Nerich, for Vince heard two more shots and was not hit. He heard Nerich's wild yelling, and there was fright in it. There was something about facing the oncoming rush of a horse that would dismay any man. He was less than a hundred yards away when Nerich's bullet struck him. It went through the fleshy part of his leg and into the horse's back. If he had been walking or standing, the shock of it would have knocked him down; mounted, he felt only the quick and piercing sting, followed by the fingers of pain running up his leg.

The horse was hit much harder. Vince felt the faltering run through it. It stumbled, almost going to its knees, and Vince leaped out of the saddle. The leg buckled under him, and he went down hard. The horse's legs folded under it, and it dropped to

the ground, threshing sideways as it did so. It made
a bulwark between Vince and Nerich, and its fall
saved Vince's life. He heard the report of the rifle
again and the following spongy thwock as the bullet
struck the horse. The horse's last rushing breath rat-
tled in its throat. It threw up its head in threshing
agony, and Vince was afraid it might get to its feet
exposing him. The energy of raising its head was all
that was left. The head fell back and except for a
quivering in its body, it was still.

Vince pressed tight against the barrel of the
animal. Nerich was on higher ground, and Vince
did not know how well the body of the horse covered him. There was no chance to crawl to better
protection. All he could do was to lay here and wait.
His leg hurt like hell, and his pant-leg was sodden
with blood. He flexed the leg, and it responded; he
thought no bone was hit. He tied his handkerchief
tightly about the wound, and that was all he could
do for now.

Nerich knew he had the advantage of position
and arms. He called tauntingly, "Come on, Carwin.
Or lay there and let the sun fry you."

"Dobie, you haven't a chance," he called in return. "They'll be looking for me in a little bit."

That should worry Nerich, he thought. He had
an equal worry. Nerich could slip away while Vince
was pinned down. He was afraid to lift his head to
see what Nerich was doing.

The minutes dragged on. Nerich might already
be gone. Or he might just be waiting for Vince to
raise his head to check on him.

Out of the corner of his left eye he caught movement, and for an instant fright's raking hand clawed him. He thought it was Nerich moving, flanking him. Then he saw it was Ceron, some five hundred yards away, moving on a sweeping, circular route to get behind Nerich.

He fired three fast, unaimed shots to keep Nerich's attention occupied, and Nerich answered with one.

"Afraid to look where you want to aim?" Nerich called, and the taunt was still in his voice. "You're gonna run out of shells, shooting that way."

"I'll have enough," Vince promised.

He kept up a sporadic fire, just enough to keep Nerich's interest pinned down. He judged he had given Ceron enough time, and he dared to take a look over the head of the dead horse. Ceron was not twenty-five yards behind Nerich. His teeth were bared, and he carried a knife. Vince thought that Ceron wanted to get close enough to use that blade.

"Why don't you give up, Dobie?" he called. "I can promise you a fair trial."

"And a rope?" Nerich chuckled. "You'll never put Dobie Nerich on the end of a rope."

Vince risked another look. Ceron had more than halved the distance separating them. It looked as though he were right behind Nerich. Ceron was moving like a drifting shadow, making not the least sound to turn Nerich's head.

"Dobie," Vince yelled. "Look behind you."

Nerich laughed. "That's an old trick, Carwin. Try something—"

"It is not a trick, fat man," a voice said softly. It sounded as though it came from right over Nerich's shoulder.

Nerich's words choked in his throat. He scrabbled about and lunged to his knees. He tried to swing the rifle muzzle to bear on the wild apparition standing before him. Ceron took a rapid stride and slashed with the blade. Its point traveled from Nerich's wrist to his elbow, and he screamed shrilly as he dropped the weapon.

He struggled to his feet, holding his slashed arm, and blood oozed between his fingers, covering his hand. He backed from the slowly advancing man. He recognized him then. It was the Indian he had questioned.

"Indian," he bleated. "You remember me. I gave you a bottle of whisky."

"I am not an Indian," Ceron said. "I am the father of the girl you hurt."

The color drained from Nerich's face, leaving it a ghastly gray. His lips looked like lines of dough, and saliva streaked his chin.

"Carwin," he bawled. "Stop him. He's got a knife. He's going to knife me. You can't let him do that to a white man."

He took another backward step and could go no farther, for a rock pressed against his back. "Carwin," he screamed again.

It was the last word he uttered. Ceron leaped at him. The blade flashed, then as it buried deep in Nerich's chest. He clawed at the shaft with both hands, trying to jerk it free. He tried to say some thing, but the rush of blood choked him. He took a forward step, then his leg buckled at the knee. He pitched forward on his face and did not move.

Ceron spat on him. "Maybe it will help Elodia a little," he muttered. He turned and moved toward Vince.

"He's dead?" Vince asked gravely.

"Much dead," Ceron said. "He knew who I was and why it was done. He lived much bad time in a few moments."

Vince nodded. Under some circumstances a man could live a lifetime in a few seconds. "I'm glad you got him," he said.

"It was fitting," Ceron gravely agreed. "You are hurt, Amigo. If you wait here, I will catch a horse."

Vince heard a distant rifle shot. He looked in its direction and said, "Hurry, Roque. It's still going on back there."

19

CERON LED the horse back toward the mouth of the arroyo. Goddard must have seen them coming from a long way off, for he began yelling before they could distinguish his words. It was some kind of a warning. The tone of his voice told them that.

Ceron said, "We stop here."

Goddard yelled again. It was broken into by the crack of a rifle. Vince held his breath. A man hit broke off like that.

Goddard resumed yelling, and Vince let go his breath. The bullet must have been close, forcing Goddard to duck. He thought, that damned rifleman is still up there. They haven't been able to get him yet. With a dismal, sinking feeling, he knew who the rifleman was. It had to be Morgan. No other of Dobie's men would have the determination or would think as fast. Instead of wild, frantic surprise overwhelming him, the man now on the higher ground had calmly worked his way there, using the first disorganized moments of the

ight to cover him. That would be Morgan, Vince
new.

Ceron said, "I go." He frowned as Vince started to
dismount. "With your bad leg, you would only slow
me. I find out what it is, then return."

"Roque, be careful. I think it's Morgan up there.
He's good with that rifle."

Ceron shrugged. "There are many rocks and
many shadows. A man must see something before
he can shoot at it."

He was gone the better part of an hour. Vince
heard a volley of shots and thought they must be
aimed at Morgan's spot, keeping him pinned, while
Ceron worked his way back. His thinking was right,
for Ceron appeared some fifteen minutes later.

"He has climbed higher than any of us," Ceron
said. "Abel tried to climb to him. Senor Goddard
thinks Abel is dead."

Vince cursed. Dan Abel with his ready humor no
matter how trying the hours that went before. You
new a man well when you worked and sweated
with him.

"Jose is bleeding from a hole in his arm." Ceron
took his head. "It is very bad. Senor Goddard says
they cannot get to him. He is afraid this man will
keep them pinned down until darkness, then climb
higher and slip over the edge. Once he does that, he
is lost."

"It won't go that long," Vince said grimly.
Morgan must be in a secure position. From his high
advantage he could cover both sides of the arroyo,
keeping men cowering behind what protective cov-
they could find. He would not risk climbing

higher or exposing himself until darkness cloaked him.

It was rough country behind the arroyo, and it would take time to work into it. He asked, "Can you get back to Goddard?"

Ceron nodded.

"Tell him to keep firing at this man. I need the sound of his shots to mark the spot for me. It'll take a couple of hours. Maybe longer."

Ceron said in quick protest, "Your bad leg, Amigo. You cannot go. I will go for you."

The leg throbbed and burned, but it would bear weight. Besides, he hoped he could ride most of the way.

He thought of Goddard and Hallie. He put a long thought on Colin. He said quietly, "The fat man belonged to you, Roque. This one belongs to me."

Ceron's shoulders rose and fell. "Some things a man has to do. Vaya con Dios."

Vince nodded and turned the horse. He moved down the valley floor toward his camp. Not more than an hour had elapsed since the fight started, but it seemed like an eternity. He washed and examined the wound. He took several steps, grimacing with each one. It would do. It would have to do.

He folded a handkerchief into a small, hard pad, placed it over the hole and bound it into place. He filled a canteen and picked up a rifle. He debated upon changing horses, then decided this one would do. He could select a faster one, but speed would be no asset in rough country.

He continued down the valley floor, looking for

assage to the rim. It had to be on the same side
Morgan was on.

He found it after a couple of miles of riding. He
et the horse pick its own way to the top, his face set
in granite lines against the weariness and pain.

He reached the top and turned back in the direc-
on he had come. He kept to the rim of the valley,
sing it as a guide. He hoped he could ride to a
pot, look down and see Morgan, and he knew it
ould not happen that way. The country was too
ough and broken. He rode around a dozen jumbles
f boulders, and twice had to leave his course to
etour around deep, small gorges. With this twist-
g and turning, a direction could be lost. He kept
stening for the sound of a rifle shot, judging he
ould be somewhere above the mouth of the ar-
yo. He heard one, faint and far away, and
owned. He was not as close as he thought he was.

He stopped and drank from the canteen and
oured half of it into his hat for the horse. The
nimal avidly drank, and Vince let it browse while
e smoked a cigarette. The leg was throbbing, and
e examined it again. Fresh blood had oozed out
ound the pad and handkerchief. Riding put a
rain on it. What would walking do?

He mounted again and continued. He hoped
oddard kept up that shooting, or otherwise he
ould never pinpoint Morgan's location.

He heard another shot, and the sound was
onger. It came from ahead and below him. He
ust be riding above the arroyo, though he could
t see it for the brush. The brush was bad here,

and in places he had to force his way through it.

He rode several hundred yards and stoppe
again, waiting for a bullet's sound. When it came
he thought it was directly ahead and below him. He
dismounted, stripped saddle and bridle from th
animal and turned it loose. He would not go bac
the way he came.

He moved toward the gash of the arroyo, makin
every step cautious and slow. It was ahead of hi,
though he could not see it.

Another rifle report changed his course a fe
degrees. Then an answering shot sounded du
ahead of him, rising out of the arroyo's depths. Th
one came from this side. He was above and behin
Morgan.

He crawled the last twenty-five yards, parted th
brush, and looked down into the arroyo. Morgan la
less than a hundred yards below him, well secure
in his nest of rocks. But he was secured from tho:
across and below him—not from a man directly b
hind and above him.

Vince cautiously worked his way over the edg
wanting to reach a position some ten yards over th
side. From where he was, he got only a partial vie
of Morgan, and the better position would lea
Morgan totally unprotected. He hoped that if Go
dard and the others saw him, they would not m:
take him for Morgan.

He moved foot by painful foot, testing each bit
ground, wanting no dislodged rock or pebble
give him away. He reached the spot he wanted, a
Morgan lay in full view. Slowly, he snuggled t

rifle butt to his shoulder. He could shoot Morgan in the back, and he did not want it that way.

"Hoyt," he called.

It looked as though Morgan went rigid before he jumped to his feet and whirled. Vince was close enough to see the trapped expression on the man's face. Vince fired as Morgan was trying to swing his rifle into line. The bullet slammed into Morgan's chest, knocking him backwards. His arms still struggled to raise the rifle, and Vince fired again.

Morgan went high on his toes, and the rifle fell from his hands. He fell over a waist-high boulder, and for a moment his body hung there. Then slowly he rolled over the boulder and disappeared from sight. Vince could hear scraping, jolting sounds as Morgan rolled down the slope.

He was suddenly bone-weary, and he doubted that at any other time in his life would he reach this point of utter spentness. It was effort to raise his voice.

"Ron," he called. "It's over."

Goddard's voice lifted to him. "I saw it, Vince. You coming down?"

"I'm coming."

It took him a long time to work his way to the bottom. The leg kept threatening to buckle on him, and he could feel stickiness of fresh bleeding.

They were grouped together, waiting for him, when he arrived. He saw no elation at the winning, only the same weariness he knew. There were fewer of them than left the camp this morning. The winning had collected its price.

"Dan?" he asked.

Goddard shook his head. "I'm afraid so, Vince."

Mendoza was cradling an arm. The sleeve of the shirt was bloodstained. "I know where he is," he said. "I will go see."

He was gone some fifteen minutes. Vince jerked in alarm at the sound of a pistol shot. "Is someone shooting at him?"

Goddard shook his head. "I don't know. I thought Morgan was the last."

Mendoza came back. Vince did not have to ask about Dan Abel. The look on Mendoza's face was answer enough.

"Was that you shooting?"

Mendoza nodded. "One of them was still alive. I heard his moaning."

He looked at the expression on Goddard's face and faintly smiled. "Senor Goddard does not approve. A matter of timing makes it wrong. A few moments ago, and any of us would have gladly shot him. Now I do it. Senor Goddard," he said softly "he could not have lived anyway."

Goddard grunted and turned toward the camp. Driscoe and Austin moved to Vince to give him support. They looked like beaten men as they straggled slowly toward the mouth of the arroyo. After they had eaten and rested, they would return for Clayton and Hall and Abel.

Mendoza and Ceron walked ahead of Vince, chattering in their native tongue. They lived closer to harsh reality than the others. This was something that had to be done, and once done could be hrugged away and forgotten.

They could break camp in the morning, Vince hought, and his face brightened. He would be anxous for that return to town. Hallie was waiting for him.

J.D. HARDIN

"THE MOST EXCITING WESTERN WRITER SINCE LOUIS L'AMOUR"
—JAKE LOGAN

____ 872-16842-5	BLOODY SANDS	$1.95
____ 867-21039-7	SONS AND SINNERS	$1.95
____ 872-16869-7	THE SPIRIT AND THE FLESH	$1.95
____ 867-21226-8	BOBBIES, BAUBLES AND BLOOD	$2.25
____ 06572-3	DEATH LODE	$2.25
____ 06138-8	HELLFIRE HIDEAWAY	$2.25
____ 06380-1	THE FIREBRANDS	$2.25
____ 06410-7	DOWNRIVER TO HELL	$2.25
____ 06001-2	BIBLES, BULLETS AND BRIDES	$2.25
____ 06331-3	BLOODY TIME IN BLACKTOWER	$2.25
____ 06248-1	HANGMAN'S NOOSE	$2.25
____ 06337-2	THE MAN WITH NO FACE	$2.25
____ 06151-5	SASKATCHEWAN RISING	$2.25
____ 06412-3	BOUNTY HUNTER	$2.50
____ 06743-2	QUEENS OVER DEUCES	$2.50
____ 07017-4	LEAD-LINED COFFINS	$2.50
____ 06845-5	SATAN'S BARGAIN	$2.50
____ 08013-7	THE WYOMING SPECIAL	$2.50
____ 07259-2	THE PECOS DOLLARS	$2.50
____ 07257-6	SAN JUAN SHOOTOUT	$2.50
____ 07379-3	OUTLAW TRAIL	$2.50
____ 07392-0	THE OZARK OUTLAWS	$2.50
____ 07461-7	TOMBSTONE IN DEADWOOD	$2.50
____ 07381-5	HOMESTEADER'S REVENGE	$2.50
____ 07386-6	COLORADO SILVER QUEEN	$2.50
____ 07790-X	THE BUFFALO SOLDIER	$2.50
____ 07785-3	THE GREAT JEWEL ROBBERY	$2.50
____ 07789-6	THE COCHISE COUNTY WAR	$2.50

Prices may be slightly higher in Canada.

B **BERKLEY**
Book Mailing Service
P.O. Box 690, Rockville Centre, NY 11571

Available at your local bookstore or return this form to.

Please send me the titles checked above. I enclose _____. Include 75¢ for postage and handling if one book is ordered; 25¢ per book for two or more not to exceed $1.75. California, Illinois, New York and Tennessee residents please add sales tax.

NAME_____

ADDRESS_____

CITY_____ STATE/ZIP_____

(allow six weeks for delivery.)

16